A S

The route Natalie had chosen led across the park, then down over a four-foot drop. Michael jumped down easily, demonstrating the athletic ease and grace that she had noted before. Strange in a man whose duties kept him inside much of the time.

She was perfectly capable of getting down, too, but she knew that the feat involved first sitting on the wall's edge—not the most graceful of acts with an interested observer standing below. She hesitated.

There was laughter in Michael's gray eyes.

"Jump," he said, holding out his arms. "I'll catch you."

Natalie thought of ignoring him but found herself unable to resist the challenge. Setting her basket down and flinging caution to the winds, she leapt from the edge and felt his muscular arms catch and hold her.

Her breath caught in her throat, and her heart started to race. Michael's arms tightened around her. He lowered his head, and for a moment she imagined that he was about to kiss her. When she had first met him, Natalie had had to reprimand him for daring to kiss her hand. She knew that she should reprove him now. He was a servant, and she was his employer.

Yet a part of her was loath to do so. She was a woman, after all. . . .

The Countess and the Butler

Elizabeth Brodnax

A SIGNET BOOK

SIGNET
Published by New American Library, a division of
Penguin Group (USA) Inc., 375 Hudson Street,
New York, New York 10014, U.S.A.
Penguin Books Ltd, 80 Strand,
London WC2R 0RL, England
Penguin Books Australia Ltd, 250 Camberwell Road,
Camberwell, Victoria 3124, Australia
Penguin Books Canada Ltd, 10 Alcorn Avenue,
Toronto, Ontario, Canada M4V 3B2
Penguin Books (NZ), cnr Rosedale and Airborne Roads,
Albany, Auckland 1310, New Zealand

Penguin Books Ltd, Registered Offices:
80 Strand, London WC2R 0RL, England

Published by Signet, an imprint of New American Library, a division of Penguin
Group (USA) Inc. This is an authorized reprint of a hardcover edition published by
Five Star in conjunction with Spectrum Literary Agency.

First Signet Printing, September 2004
10 9 8 7 6 5 4 3 2 1

For Susan C. Stone,
who believed in this book.
Sue, if it hadn't been for your help,
encouragement and matchless advice,
this book might never have seen the light of day.

Chapter One

"**A** prince of Estavia become *what?*" exclaimed Josef Stern, his outraged voice rising shrilly. The crisp German words reverberated off the walls of the little bedchamber at the Fox and Hare, the sole inn gracing the tiny Cotswold village of Abbingford Magna. "Are my ears, perhaps, deceiving me?"

The man to whom he was talking, His Highness Prince Michael Rupert Franz Peter von Stell of Estavia, sat sprawled in the single comfortable chair in the room, pretending complete indifference to the matter that was causing his longtime servant such outrage. Only one booted foot, nervously tapping the floor, betrayed him.

"You heard me correctly, Josef. I think my seeking gainful employment would solve all our problems," he replied, also in German. Michael was fluent in English, for his paternal grandmother had been an English noblewoman, but when he spoke with Josef they always lapsed into the comfortable familiarity of Estavian-accented German.

"A prince of Estavia taking monetary remuneration . . ." Josef's voice was filled with tragic woe. "And worse yet, taking a position as a *servant!*"

"An upper servant, Josef. A butler, in fact. The most senior of all the household staff."

"That such a day should ever dawn . . ." mourned Josef. "If the Prince your father were alive to see this—"

"He is not," said Michael in a quelling voice.

"Prince Carl Friedrich, then," continued Josef, unfazed. "*He* would not demean the House of Stell in such a way."

"I have no wish to discuss my half brother Carl Friedrich. He may be our father's oldest son, and thus the ruler of Estavia, but he's certainly not infallible," snapped Michael. "If it were not for him, I wouldn't be here in the first place. I would be home in comfort in Stellberg, not driven to seek a position as a butler in England."

Josef looked at the man who had been his responsibility for twenty-four years now, ever since Josef was appointed body servant to the toddling child. He was certainly not a child any longer, even if Josef was sometimes betrayed into scolding him as if he were one. He was twenty-six years old, in the prime of manhood. Six foot one, lean yet well-muscled, with midnight-black hair, and eyes the unfathomable pale gray of a steel sword, he was strikingly handsome. Even now that he was exiled from Estavia, women still looked at him with interest and approval. But that did not mean that Josef always approved of his actions, especially if he felt that his prince was not being properly conscious of his royal rank, as he did now.

He grunted crossly. "I never should have mentioned that the position of butler was open at Amesworth Court, but it certainly did not occur to me that you would contemplate demeaning yourself in such a way. Why should you do so? Do you not feel I am earning enough as Mr. Chesney's valet to support us both? I realize that it is not in the manner to which you are accustomed, my prince, but surely it is sufficient."

Michael sighed. "Josef, my very dear Josef, do you

think I care in what style I live? And I know you would continue to support me forever if need be. But I cannot allow you to do so. It's been five months now since we left Estavia, and I still have not received a single word from Carl Friedrich. I'm beginning to believe that he must have decided to cut me off for good. And you haven't heard the latest news yet."

He pulled a crumpled sheet of paper from his pocket. "I may not have heard from Carl Friedrich, but poor Toni has. She received this just before I visited her in Bath."

He smoothed out the mistreated letter. "Listen to our revered ruler's newest dictum to my little sister. 'My dearest Antonia,' then, blah, blah, blah . . . Carl Friedrich's typical pomposities. Oh, here we go. . . . 'I am sure you will be as honored as I am when you hear that I have received a flattering offer for your hand from the Emperor Napoleon himself, who wishes you to wed his cousin Orlando Bonaparte.'"

Michael snorted. "Boney has run out of brothers and sisters to marry off to the royalty of Europe, so now he's moving on to cousins. Anyway, Carl Friedrich continues: 'The details of the marriage treaty have not yet been settled, but I anticipate that your wedding will take place in late fall or early winter, since the emperor expects to be involved in military campaigns throughout the summer. I hope you will join with me in rejoicing over this profoundly advantageous alliance for Estavia. When I have further news, I will send for you to return home. Until then, you will oblige me by remaining, as you have in past years, at your school in Bath.'"

Michael wadded the letter up into a ball again. "'Flattering' . . . 'advantageous,'" he quoted bitterly. "Carl Friedrich and I have quite different ideas on the subject of Napoleon Bonaparte. That's why I'm here, after all, rather than back in Estavia. But I never thought that even

Carl Friedrich would go so far as to promise to ally a member of the Estavian royal family to that Corsican upstart. It doesn't seem to occur to Carl Friedrich that poor Toni might not *want* to be married to some middle-class merchant.

"Of course," he mused aloud, "she's always known she'd have to marry for Estavia's interests . . . but to a relative of Bonaparte? I think not. Antonia tells me that she has no wish for such a union, and I will not let her be sacrificed in this way. Thank heaven she's still here in England. And thank heaven I am here to counsel and encourage her. There's not much that Carl Friedrich can do if Toni refuses to return to Estavia. Except, of course, cut off all funds to her, meager as they have been to date. So it is absolutely imperative that I find some way to earn a living in order to provide for her.

"I'd like to join the British army, strike a blow against Napoleon myself, since Carl Friedrich won't let our country do so, but I haven't the money for a commission. Anyway, I daren't risk my life with Toni's future in such question. Maybe we can persuade Carl Friedrich to give up on this ridiculous espousal. Or maybe if we stall long enough, Bonaparte will marry off his damn cousin to some other poor princess."

Under such an onslaught of impassioned oration, Josef capitulated. Despite his strong sense of what was due a prince of Estavia, he cared first and foremost for the man he had seen grow from childhood to maturity. He was willing to attempt whatever would make his master happy. If that meant assisting him to become a servant, then so be it.

"It must be as my prince wishes," he said quietly. "At least I can console myself that if you were to become the butler to a countess, some respect would be accorded you."

Michael laughed. "I suppose. It is good to see you again, Josef. I've missed you."

He frowned, thinking of the months they had been separated. Their finances had run precariously low immediately following their hurried exile from Estavia in January, so when Josef had revealed his intent to take a position with a Mr. Maximilian Chesney, who had advertised for a valet in the *Times*, Michael had not argued. Josef, at least, would live in some comfort, then.

Michael hadn't expected, however, Josef's job to be on the far edge of the Cotswolds. It was not all that distant from London, but neither man had the funds to spare for coach trips around the English countryside. Michael hadn't even been able to visit his sister, Antonia, in Bath until Josef sent him the greater part of his first quarter's wages.

When he realized that Abbingford Magna could be said, by only a slight stretch of the imagination, to be on the way back from Bath, he had leapt at the chance to look in on Josef. He had taken a room at the Fox and Hare and, posing as a cousin of Josef's, sent word to Amesworth Court, where his manservant was now employed, asking if Josef could get leave to see him. The resulting visit was pleasant, but it was Josef's casual mention that Amesworth Court lacked a butler that gave Michael his astonishing idea—one he immediately presented to Josef. Michael had always believed that following ideas with action produced the best results.

He might be that ridiculous cipher, a prince-in-exile, but he was not completely lacking in practical skills, as those of his ilk often were. His had been a lonely childhood—his parents aloof and occupied with matters of state, his half brother Carl Friedrich fourteen years older, and his beloved sister Antonia not born until Michael was nearly eight. He had beguiled away many of those early years, spent in his family's country residence, Schloss Stell, by frequenting the servants' halls. He thought he had some idea of how a well-regulated princely household in a German state was run. Surely the English nobility did not comport themselves all that differently. If he took a position in service, he could support himself and Antonia until either he reconciled with Carl Friedrich or a better solution came to him, which surely it would. He had faith in that.

"Will you give me your help, then, in obtaining this position, Josef?" he asked. "To whom do I need to submit my application?"

"Well . . . it really should be the dowager countess, odd though that may sound," said Josef slowly, giving the matter some thought. "Things are at sixes and sevens at Amesworth Court and have been for some time. The old earl died nearly a year ago, but his widow has remained in residence. They didn't have any children, so the new earl is the son of a deceased cousin of the old earl. He has been living on the island of Jamaica for nearly a decade, and the dowager is waiting for him to arrive so that he can make whatever household decisions he wishes. He's expected to show up within a month or so, I believe."

"I should speak to the dowager, then?"

"That would be the proper course of action," replied Josef, "but I think it would serve you better to speak first with my employer, Mr. Maximilian Chesney."

"Why on earth would I do that?" Michael asked. "Who exactly is he?"

"He's another cousin of the late earl, though he's not in the direct line of succession. He's been at the Court since he was a child. He has some money—sufficient to pay for his fancy clothes and a valet—but not enough to support an establishment of his own if he wishes to live in style, which he definitely does. So he remains at Amesworth instead."

"But why would I speak with him? Does he run the household?"

"Well, I think there was an idea at one point that he would assist with the management of the estate, though that didn't come to much. However, in this case, he's the one who feels that Amesworth should not remain even temporarily without a butler, and he asked me if I knew of anyone. I think he has some new scheme in mind, as he often does, though I'm not quite sure what it is this time."

"So it would be best if I spoke with him," Michael summarized. "Let me think. . . . I'm going to need a name. And some references . . ." He grinned. "I should think a reference for Michael Schmidt, butler, from Prince Michael of Estavia, might serve."

"It should serve very well, indeed, my prince."

Michael scowled slightly. "Now, that's something that will have to go."

Josef looked startled. "What must go, my prince?"

"You'll have to stop calling me that."

"Calling you what, my prince?"

" 'My prince.' You'll have to stop it. Do you think you could perhaps get your tongue around 'Michael'? And do you think you could arrange for me to speak with your Mr. Chesney?"

"Yes, I think I could do that, my pr—"

Michael frowned awfully at him.

"I mean, yes . . . Michael," said Josef, but he was unable to repress the look of dismay that crossed his face as he pronounced the prince's baptismal name.

Michael sighed. He had already envisioned all sorts of possible hazards, but he was starting to suspect that the hardest part of his upcoming effort might be persuading Josef to forgo this small formality.

Chapter Two

Some days were just too nice to be immured indoors, thought Natalie Chesney, the dowager Countess of Amesworth. Today was a beautiful day, and she longed to be outside in it, dancing and singing with the jubilant birds. That was something she had done far too seldom in recent years—indeed, not since her pretty, impetuous, French-born mother, who died so young, had whisked her out to play childish games in the meadows.

This past year she had been inside altogether too much, imprisoned not only by the four walls of the house but also by the furious grief she had felt when her husband, Alden, died. For many, many months her chief emotion had been sheer, overwhelming anger at fate's unjust course. If she were a melodramatic sort, she would have wailed that anybody she came to care for was always taken from her.

It hadn't been fair for Alden, either, of course, and she had felt a great deal of anger about that, as well. When she met him, he had been in his early fifties. Despite the more than thirty years that lay between them in age, she had not thought it an unreasonable marriage, for after the death of her first love, the young army officer Giles Hunter, Natalie had not wanted to fall in love again. Alden Chesney was not merely the sixth Earl of

Amesworth. He was also a hale, hearty, athletic man who still loved to ride to hounds and drive his own horses. He was, in fact, a more dependable version of the dashing father she had lost, along with her mother, in a tragic carriage accident that had occurred while she was still very young. Natalie had adored Alden, and resented bitterly that a stroke of apoplexy rendered him a hopeless invalid a mere two days after their marriage. Crueler still was his long, slow death.

Of late, though, Natalie had surprised herself by beginning to smile once again. Just as surely as spring and summer followed winter, her terrible grief was finally receding. True, that had happened before, but the depths of her rage and despair after so many losses, culminating in Alden's death, had made her unable to accept that possibility.

After Giles had died in the war in Spain, Alden had been the man who had brought some happiness back into her life. Because her guardian—her uncle James—had considered Giles a penniless nobody, she had never been formally engaged, although she had considered herself promised. Uncle James and Aunt Emilia had not allowed her the merciful respite of mourning, but had forced her to continue to entertain suitors and attend the endless round of balls that Season. For a while it had seemed intolerable. Then Alden Chesney, with his wry humor and his fatherly compassion for her grief, had offered her an escape.

This time, though, Alden was the one who had died, and there was no one to comfort her. At least, however, as a widow, she was afforded the expected trappings and seclusion and found they provided her blessed relief.

Now, slowly, she was finding pleasure in little things. She still rarely went out and about, but a few months ago she had discarded her black dresses for the paler grays and lavenders of half mourning. Soon, she thought, she would leave off the mourning altogether. She also knew her smile was not just brave and bright but genuine once again. She was settling into the role of dowager countess—her final gift from Alden.

The rhythm and routines of country life felt right to her, and she was looking forward to her upcoming move to the dower house, which she wished to accomplish just as soon as the new earl and his wife arrived from Jamaica. While she was proud of her ability to run a nobleman's mansion in a proper and elegant fashion, she thought it would be fun to have a little house that was all her own, with only a couple of servants. Perhaps she could even grow a small garden.

With a start, Natalie realized she had been staring out the window at nothing for quite some minutes. She would never accomplish the move to the dower house if she continued to daydream. Sighing, she looked down at her list of tasks, blank thus far, on the French marquetry escritoire. She had left word with the staff that she would be in the boudoir adjacent to her bedchamber and should not be summoned except for emergencies. She was determined not only to finish her list this morning, but also to attend to several other matters that had been awaiting her consideration for far too long.

Items Needing Attention at Dower House, she wrote in the neat copperplate script that had been drummed into her at Miss Mendip's Academy for Young Ladies. After considering this heading for several minutes, she drew a heavy black line under it, then gazed out the window again. The wide stretch of green lawn sloped down to the sparkling waters of the lake, luring her. She loved the lake here at Amesworth.

She checked herself, realizing she still had accomplished nothing. She must be more focused.

"Choose new material for drawing room drapes. Damask or velvet?" she murmured triumphantly to herself. With a flourish, she wrote down this first project. Perhaps if she finished her list soon, she could walk down to the gardens by the lake.

A sound behind her made her jump. She turned to see Maximilian Chesney's slightly pixie-like face peering around the door leading to the corridor.

"Am I disturbing you, Natalie?" he asked.

Annoyed at the interruption, she would have loved to snap, *Yes, you are, and not knocking doesn't mitigate the disturbance.* She hated to hurt Max's feelings, though. He honestly meant well. So instead she merely said, "Hello, Cousin Max. Please, come in."

He entered the room fully, closing the door behind him.

Natalie eyed him a trifle uneasily, for she recognized the look on his face. It was the one reminiscent of a cat that has eaten a canary. She fancied she could see a little yellow feather or two sticking to his chin. Unfortunately, whenever Cousin Max got notions, they always threw Natalie's life into disorder.

Since Max had resided at Amesworth far longer than she had, she had no desire to deny his right to treat the Court as his home, but she wished he wouldn't interfere so often in her affairs. In theory, Max helped the professional estate agent manage Amesworth Court and the farms and other properties owned by the earldom. In practice, he showed neither talent for nor interest in this occupation and had long since abandoned those mundane matters. Instead, Max devoted his energy to pursuing clever schemes for the good of the Chesney family. Sadly, the altruistic nature of these schemes did little to diminish the confusion they caused.

Regarding Max's portly, fashionably dressed form,

Natalie ran a frustrated hand through her already tousled curls.

"I thought you had gone into the village," she said. She had been delighted at breakfast when Max had announced his plan to do so, thinking that his absence would offer her the peace she needed to complete her own tasks.

"I did, but I finished my errand expeditiously, so I thought I would visit with you, my dear. I've asked Percy to bring up some tea and cold meats."

"Max, I'm rather busy and not very hungry," she said, more curtly than was perhaps polite. She turned back to her list, because the mention of food had reminded her of something.

"Install closed stove in kitchen," she murmured to herself as she wrote. The dower house had not been occupied since Alden's mother died fifteen years previously, and its furnishings and equipment were sadly outmoded.

She looked up again. "Max, I told you just last week that I received a letter from the new earl. He's finally arranged his affairs in Jamaica to his liking and will be returning to England by the end of August. I'm determined to be out of this house by that time, and the dower house is nowhere near fit to live in. I really must get this list done today." She sighed. "Of course, I should have started months ago, but it seemed so distant then." She studied her list, frowning, her attention only partly on Max. "I know there's something I'm supposed to be remembering."

Max sat down in a chair beside her desk. "I sent out invitations for a house party this morning, Natalie."

Natalie jumped. "What?" Now he had her attention. "A house party! Max, surely you are not serious. Please, please, tell me you're jesting."

"Not a very big party," Max said. "Only eight or ten guests."

"Only eight or ten!" Natalie echoed, her voice rising to a squeak. "Cousin Max, how could you even think of filling the house with guests when I'm preparing to move? Besides, I'm not out of mourning for Alden yet."

"It's been nearly a year. And you're only in half mourning now," Max pointed out. He surveyed Natalie's pale gray muslin round gown, tied with a lilac-colored sash. "I'm sure it would be perfectly permissible to have a small party next month, once you're out of mourning altogether. Why, it's so tiny a group, it hardly counts as a party at all. Anyway, if you're determined to be such a stickler for the proprieties, you may reassure yourself that I, not you, invited them."

"But how could you do such a thing, Max?" Natalie protested. "Now, of all times? Couldn't you have waited until I was safely settled in the dower house?"

"Safely *immured* in the dower house," Max retorted roundly, "where you'll never see anyone except the local fuddy-duddies. You're barely past twenty. You've not had a chance to enjoy life. Will you be going up to Town for the Season next year?"

"I don't know. I haven't thought that far ahead. It would be terribly complicated. Heaven knows the jointure Alden left me is certainly more than adequate, but I'd have to rent a house because the new earl will presumably want to use Amesworth House. Then I'd have to staff it, and I shudder to think of all the bother that entails. . . . Anyway, Cousin Lucretia's health is not really up to London, and I certainly couldn't go without my companion. I don't know, Max. Probably not."

"That's exactly what I mean, Natalie. Think of the Seasons you missed because Alden was ill and then because you were in mourning. You're young yet, Natalie. You can't let life pass you by."

She smiled wryly. "I am the dowager Countess of

Amesworth. I have a handsome competence, a very nice residence once I find the time to make it habitable, and a role in life to play. Not to mention that I like the countryside and the local fuddy-duddies very much. I'll be quite happy in the dower house."

"Well, you shouldn't be," Max said robustly. "It's wrong. It's . . . it's unnatural, that's what it is."

Natalie's wry expression turned to a twinkle. "Poor Cousin Max, have you been longing to make a bolt to Town? I wouldn't stop you, you know, and I'm sure the new earl would not object if you wished to open up Amesworth House."

Max looked indignant. "Dash it, Natalie, what good would that do? It's the end of June already. You know better than that. Anybody who is anybody in the *ton* will be gone in another week or so. I'll be lucky if my invitations catch everyone."

"Ah, yes, the invitations," said Natalie dryly. "I suppose there's no hope of retrieving them now."

"They went out on the eleven o'clock mail coach. I handed them to the guard myself," said Max, smug satisfaction apparent in his voice. "Not a hope."

"Well, Max, I really don't want to quarrel with you. But you do seem to have overlooked several important points," Natalie said. "And the last one could be a genuine problem. Have you considered what we are to do about a butler if we have guests to stay? It's one thing to manage without a butler when just you and Lucretia and I are here, but we certainly could not have a house party without one. And I've already got quite enough on my hands trying to ready the dower house, without worrying about adding to the staff at this point."

Max's face revealed a mixture of apprehension and triumph. "Well, as to that, I've found you a butler."

"*Max!*" Natalie said, rising to her feet. She did not

usually allow Max's interfering ways to distress her overly much, but enough was enough. "You know as well as I do that I had decided we would effect no unnecessary changes in the staff until the new earl and his countess arrived. I don't want to make such important decisions for them. And, speaking of important decisions, what right— what possible right—do you think you have to find a butler for me? And have you merely found him, or have you hired him as well?"

Max looked uncomfortable. "Well, I didn't exactly hire . . . I mean, I know I have no authority . . . But I'm afraid I did rather lead him to expect . . ."

Natalie sighed and sat back down, her bout of ill temper passing as quickly as it had come. "Don't look so woebegone, Cousin Max. What's done is done, I suppose." Then she shook her head. "I'm sorry. I don't mean to sound so grudging, but I'm not sure you understand what a strain all this is for me, trying to plan my own move and keep Amesworth Court running smoothly at the same time."

"But don't you think a new butler will solve some of your problems?" Max asked eagerly.

Natalie thought it was equally likely that any butler chosen by Cousin Max might create more problems than he solved. However, it was always pointless to argue with Max when he was convinced he was right. Accepting the inevitable with as much grace as she could, she smiled kindly. "I hope so. Who is this man, anyway? Did you get references?"

"Stern—you know my valet Josef Stern—informed me of him. His name is Michael Schmidt. He has a truly impeccable background. He was butler to the royal family of Estavia at their *schloss* in the country, and, like Josef himself, he has a reference from Prince Michael of Estavia."

"Estavia?" echoed Natalie, distracted from the topic under discussion. "I hadn't realized your valet was Estavian. What a strange coincidence. I was at school in Bath, at Miss Mendip's Academy, with Princess Antonia of Estavia. I believe Prince Michael is her elder brother. Poor little Antonia. She was only twelve and very homesick. I was several years older and about to leave Miss Mendip's, but we became quite close. I think Antonia saw me as an older sister. I haven't seen her since then, but we still correspond. I just received a letter from her, in fact. She's seventeen now, but is staying on at the academy, at least for the summer. I believe the political situation in Estavia is difficult at present, which is why she has not returned home, but I'm not sure. She said something, too, about her brother and half brother having quarreled, but I'm afraid I didn't follow that part at all. Antonia is not always clear on these points. Actually, I'd been thinking how delightful it would be to see her again before she returns to Estavia."

"Well, then," said Max triumphantly, "invite her to the house party. You will have a chance to renew your acquaintance, and she will have a chance to see her family's old butler. It will be a link with home for her, if she's so homesick."

Natalie laughed. "She's not homesick now, Max. It's been five years, and she's become a grown lady. But maybe I should invite her. I would like to see Antonia again. Oh, and, Max . . . ?"

"Yes," said Max hopefully.

"You'd better send word to this butler of yours that he should come to see me. Where is he? In the village, I suppose. I presume that's what you were up to this morning, after you mailed the invitations."

Max shifted uncomfortably, then recognized the twinkle in Natalie's eyes. He relaxed. "Yes," he confessed, "it was."

"So, send a message that he should come up here to speak with me. After all—" she paused portentously "—we are going to have to train him to our ways before this house party, aren't we?"

Max nodded in relief. "You're not going to regret this, Natalie, I promise. Believe me, this house party is the very answer to all your problems." He turned to leave the room, coming as close to skipping as a man of his girth could achieve.

"Problems?" asked Natalie. "What problems?"

But Max merely held a coy finger to his lips as he closed the door gently behind himself.

Josef came down to the Fox and Hare to deliver the news to Prince Michael in person.

"Mr. Chesney has persuaded the dowager countess to hire you. But she does want to speak with you in person first. You're to come up tomorrow morning, she says."

"So you were right," Michael said. "It was best to approach Mr. Chesney first. Don't you think that is odd, though, Josef?"

"Very odd," said Josef, "but that's the way things are run of late at Amesworth Court. I may have been there scarcely three months, but it didn't take me long to get a pretty good idea of the way things work. When Mr. Maximilian Chesney gets it into his head to do something, he just does it. He's not one to think about should or shouldn't, if you'll pardon my saying so, but the countess rarely gainsays him. Apparently the old earl, his cousin, let him do pretty much as he pleased, and the dowager countess prefers to continue respecting her husband's wishes in that matter."

"What's the dowager like?" asked Michael idly. "Typical ugly old bird, I suppose."

At that moment Josef conceived a splendid idea. It

grieved him sorely to see his royal master struggling for subsistence, and this latest determination to become a servant was the most distressing development of all. But what if some good were to come of it? A countess was not a princess, of course. But England, unlike the German states, seemed to have a serious shortage of princesses. The dowager Countess of Amesworth was young and lovely, and gossip in the servants' hall, which was usually highly accurate, indicated that she possessed a considerable jointure that would not disappear if she remarried.

Josef had no doubts that the countess would find his master attractive. That lean yet sinewy frame, the hint of coiled strength even when the prince was in repose, was irresistibly attractive to women. Of course, he showed to best advantage in the silver-braided uniform and plumed shako of an Estavian army officer, astride a mettlesome horse, but Michael Rupert Franz Peter von Stell did not truly need such trappings to catch the eye. Josef was confident that if his prince so wished, he could readily attract the countess.

So despite the brilliance of his idea, Josef maintained an impassive expression. "She is very kind and gentlehearted," was all he said, congratulating himself on implying agreement with the prince's assessment by what he omitted. Let the prince discover for himself what the dowager countess was like. Perhaps the surprise of learning that his employer-to-be was a lovely young woman would put him into a properly romantic frame of mind.

"Well," said Michael, dismissing the subject without a second thought, "let's just hope she's kind and gentlehearted enough to second Mr. Chesney's decision to hire me."

Chapter Three

Michael smiled as he strode up the tree-lined drive leading through the great park that sat between the village of Abbingford Magna and Amesworth Court. It was a perfect day for walking—a beautiful summer morning, soft and misty with a balminess that promised warmth later, when the sun burned off the fog. In front of him, across gently rolling lawns that he guessed had been designed by Capability Brown or one of that eminent designer's disciples, a low-lying lake was still shrouded in the early mists. A graceful marble bridge crossed it at the far end, and a grassy promontory jutting into it was crowned by an exquisite copy of a Grecian temple. All around him grew carefully tended woods and copses of rhododendron.

Suddenly becoming poor had its compensations, he decided. It would have been a shame to be imprisoned in a carriage on such a day. Josef had warned him that it was more than two miles from the village, which stood at the gates of the park, to the house, but Michael had often covered greater distances in far rougher territory in his own mountains when he hunted chamois. This perfectly graded gravel drive, winding along the edge of gently rolling hills, posed no challenge to him.

It was, however, very beautiful and, to sensibilities attuned to the majesty of the German Alps, very exotic. He began to whistle one of his favorite passages from Beethoven's Pastoral Symphony. He had been extremely impressed by Herr Beethoven's music for a number of years. In fact, after hearing the Pastoral Symphony three years before at its premiere in Vienna, he had persuaded the composer to conduct a performance of it in Stellberg.

As he followed the drive, Amesworth Court appeared from behind a fold in the hills. Michael nodded in approval. It was not nearly so grand as his family's country home, Schloss Stell, of course, but it was an imposing edifice. Built of pale cream Cotswold stone in the classic Palladian mode, it was a striking modern house—fifty or sixty years old, at most, he guessed. He particularly admired the pillared portico. His father had ordered the palace in Stellberg remodeled in a similar style when Michael was a baby.

He rounded the lake and continued the last half mile up the drive. As Josef had instructed, he followed the graveled carriage sweep around to the back of the house and through a stone archway into the stable yard.

A young fellow—presumably a footman, although it was hard to tell, since he was in his shirtsleeves and holding a silver fork and a polishing rag in one hand—answered Michael's knock at the staff entrance.

"Good morning," Michael said cheerfully in the fluent English he had learned as a child from his grandmother. "My name's Michael Schmidt. The dowager countess sent word down to the village yesterday that she wished to see me this morning."

"Oh, yes, Mr. Schmidt, her ladyship is expecting you. Please come in. Her ladyship requested I take you directly to her in the library." He turned to lead the way, but not before giving Michael a quick, assessing glance.

It was not surprising that the footman was curious,

thought Michael as he followed him along the wide stone-flagged passage. Josef would not have volunteered any information, but Michael knew the kind of communication that existed among the servants of a large household. Someone undoubtedly had overheard something, and by evening yesterday the entire staff would have known that there was talk of hiring a new butler. They must have been wondering what he would be like.

"Excuse me, Mr. Schmidt," the footman said. "I'll be back in a moment." He ducked into a room off the passage, returning without the cutlery or cleaning rag and shrugging into his frogged blue velvet coat. He then led the way up a narrow staircase, through a green baize door, and along a white-paneled corridor into the front hall. Michael looked about in appreciation, for the square hall, too, was a lovely example of the Palladian style. Quietly elegant rather than grandiose in any way, it featured an unusual floor—patterned in squares of black and white marble—and a graceful split staircase that framed the front entrance, then ascended the side walls to a second-floor balcony.

Michael wondered again about the dowager countess. He wished he could question this young man, but such an act would be detrimental to his future authority as butler if he were hired. He must not appear nervous.

Well, he was considered to have a way with ladies, young and old. Besides, his English grandmother had been a holy terror, but Michael had usually managed to stay in her good graces. Surely the dowager Countess of Amesworth, even if she were an elderly harridan, could be no worse.

The footman walked through a door that stood ajar on one side of the hall and stood back, revealing a well-proportioned room. Along the left wall, sunshine poured through tall windows facing the carriage sweep. Bookcases filled with leather-bound volumes lined the other walls. But Michael gave the library only the most cursory glance, for his attention was immediately drawn elsewhere.

On the far side of the room stood a massive mahogany desk, and balancing precariously atop it was a lovely young lady dressed in a demure cambric dress. She was engaged in taking down a stack of document boxes from a shelf above her head. As she did so, she revealed an exceptionally fine pair of ankles.

Michael stared in masculine appreciation.

Behind him, the footman coughed discreetly.

The young lady started and began to turn toward the door. The topmost box in her pile began to slip, and as she tried to secure it, she lost her footing and teetered dangerously at the edge of the desk.

Instantly Michael moved across the room and reached up to clasp her slender waist and steady her.

"Watch my boxes," she said breathlessly, and, indeed, the pile was wobbling dangerously.

The young footman was now at Michael's elbow.

"Take the boxes, man," Michael ordered sharply, his princely instinct to command leaping to the fore.

The footman grasped the leather-covered boxes and retreated a few paces.

Michael effortlessly swung the girl down from the desk. He set her squarely on her feet, but made no move to release her. Instead, he stood, looking down into her face. She was quite the most enchanting minx he had ever seen in his life. Her reddish gold curls, trailing appealingly from a high knot, perfectly set off her rose-petal skin and her enormous, blue-gray eyes. Below the demure white collar of the soft, smoky gray cambric morning dress she wore, her breast heaved with her rapid breathing, and her soft pink lips were parted slightly.

Who was she? he wondered. A granddaughter of the dowager, perhaps? But, no, Josef had mentioned that the dowager was childless. The companion, then. Josef had definitely spoken of a companion. That must be who she was. A shame that such charm and innocence should be wasted in attendance on an elderly lady.

He tightened his grasp slightly. The temptation to kiss her was nearly overwhelming. However, as a prince and a gentleman it was his rule neither to take advantage of the lower orders nor to raise unreasonable expectations. Certainly a lady's companion was not a suitable match for a prince of Estavia. But perhaps a little dalliance would not harm anyone. Those enchanting lips, that glimpse of a delicate, shell-like ear beneath the curls— they were almost irresistible.

The footman moved past him to lay the document boxes on the desk, and Michael started. He had forgotten the young fellow's presence.

"I hope you have not come to any harm, your ladyship," said the footman.

Your ladyship! Michael's hands fell to his sides, and he stared, stunned, at the girl standing before him. This young beauty couldn't possibly be the dowager countess?

"I'm quite fine, Oliver," the girl replied softly. She took a deep breath. "You must be the applicant for the position of butler," she said to Michael, her voice now crisp and sure.

Merciful heavens, she *was* the dowager countess. Michael struggled to assemble his thoughts. How astounding! Why hadn't Josef warned him?

He knew he was gaping like an idiot. He knew he had to do something. He just didn't know what. Without thought, he reacted with the courtly manners that were bred in the bone with him.

"Countess, I am your very humble servant," he said,

taking her hand. With a sharp, Germanic click of his heels, he bowed low over her fingers, raising them to his lips. Since they had only just met, propriety dictated that his lips merely hover above her skin, but the soft touch of her fingers on his and the delicate scent of lavender were irresistible. He pressed his lips gently to her hand.

She gasped.

He released her hand and looked up.

She took a few steps backward, placing distance between them.

"Schmidt, I think you forget yourself!" she said reprovingly.

As if dashed by a bucket of cold water, Michael remembered that he was supposed to be a butler, not a prince. This was not how servants acted toward the ruling class. If he wanted this job, he was going to have to think quickly.

"Countess," he said, forcing a puzzled, innocent frown to his face, "is something wrong? How have I offended you?"

She stared at him, nonplused. "I am not used to such . . ." She faltered. "Is this how servants in Europe greet their employers?"

Michael fought to restrain a grin at the thought. His deceased Prussian mother would have instantly exiled a servant who indulged in such an unforgivable intimacy and would have thought it a pity that these modern, more informal times no longer permitted execution for such offenses.

"Absolutely, countess," he said solemnly, seizing upon the excuse.

"I see," said the young dowager uncertainly. With visible effort, she recovered herself. "I would appreciate it, however, if you refrained from such gestures in future. They are not considered appropriate here in England."

She moved behind the large desk and sat down, every movement a studied barrier against further intimacy.

"Oliver, you may leave us now," she said to the gaping young footman.

As Oliver, his mouth still ajar, departed, the dowager countess looked down at a document on the desk. Michael recognized it as the recommendation he had written for himself.

"Mr. Schmidt," she said, an enchanting tinge of rose staining her cheeks, "I am sure England and its customs must still be strange to you, but you do come very highly recommended. And Mr. Chesney was extremely impressed when he spoke with you. But . . . how long were you a butler at Schloss Stell? I must admit I had expected someone slightly older."

You *expected someone older!*, Michael thought fervently. *Damn you, Josef! Why didn't you warn me?*

"Mr. Schmidt?"

He realized he hadn't answered her question. "I was the butler for only a few years, milady," he said mechanically. "But I was . . . in service at Schloss Stell for many years before that. Since I was a boy, in fact."

He paused, trying to regain his equilibrium. Thank heaven he had rehearsed his answers at some length with Josef, so he could produce them now without much conscious thought or excessive untruthfulness.

"I knew the old butler there very well," he added. "I think I can presume to say I was a favorite of his." That last was certainly true. Old Hermann had been devoted to him. Most of his story was true, in fact, although he neglected to mention the trivial fact that his family owned Schloss Stell.

"So you were learning at a master's knee," said the countess, as if encouraging a reticent schoolboy.

Dash it, this was ridiculous. She was treating him as if

she were the adult and he the child. He'd be damned if this chit was more than a year past Antonia's seventeen. But, no, she must be older than that. Josef had told him that her husband was dead nearly a year now, so unless she had been a child bride . . .

The countess was smiling at him expectantly. Michael hastily reassembled his thoughts. They had been talking about old Hermann at Schloss Stell.

"He was a very fine butler, milady. The prince and princess demanded a great deal of ceremony when they were in residence at the palace in Stellberg, but Schloss Stell was their country home. Also, the prince's mother was an English lady. Although she could not alter the royal ceremony in Stellberg, she had very definite ideas of how Schloss Stell should be run. Before the war, we had many English visitors, and they frequently commented how much it reminded them of home."

The countess smiled. "That certainly sounds very satisfactory. Well, since Mr. Chesney has already indicated to you that you might have the position, I am merely confirming his offer. Are you still interested?"

Was he interested? Oh, merciful heavens, he was definitely interested! But not, exactly, in the position of butler. When she smiled that way, her blue eyes sparkled like star sapphires, and her lips held the most inviting curve.

He came to himself with a snap. If he were to play the role of butler successfully, such thoughts must be suppressed. Of course she had not meant her smile to hold any sort of invitation. She had already made it clear to him that he was a servant and she too far above him even to consider him as a man. She believed the distance between them greater than it would have been between a prince of Estavia and the lady's companion he had first thought her. If she had truly been a mere companion, then perhaps—if he were the household butler—they might have formed a romantic attachment, but she had been offended when he merely kissed her hand.

Despite his financial problems and his concern over Antonia, becoming a butler for a few months had seemed almost a lark to him. But the drawbacks, though not necessarily those that had been apparent to Josef, were becoming clear to him, too. To be a servant to a woman he would desire every time he saw her . . . The idea was agony. Servants weren't supposed to have feelings, especially ones like that. He would be a fool to place himself in such a predicament.

If he had any sense at all, he would walk away from Amesworth Court and never return. However, there was Antonia to be considered. Also, he had never backed down when danger threatened. And how many other ready chances would he get for the gainful employment he needed?

"Yes, your ladyship, I would be pleased to serve you," Michael found himself saying.

A worried frown entered her blue eyes. "I must tell you—I don't know if Mr. Chesney made this clear to you—that we are a household in transition. I will be moving to the dower house shortly, and I cannot guarantee you a position here when the new earl returns at the end of the summer. I hope he will not make many changes, but he and his wife may have ideas of their own on the employment of the staff. I am afraid I cannot promise you continued employment."

"That is not a problem, milady," said Michael quickly. While he could see that so uncertain a future could be dismaying to a real servant wishful of obtaining stable employment, he certainly had no intention of remaining a butler any longer than necessary. The end of the summer might suit him very well. Perhaps by then he would have found another solution to his dilemma, perhaps even found some terms of agreement with Carl Friedrich.

"I am sure everything will be satisfactory," he said.

She smiled in evident relief. "Then you are decided. You will take the position."

"Yes, milady."

"Well," she said, "I am pleased. I feel sure you will be a success." She tugged on the bell pull beside her, then returned her attention to Michael. "When can you start?"

"I would need to fetch my belongings from London, milady, but I could return directly after that."

"Good." She turned to the door as a footman—not the one who had originally escorted Michael—opened it. "Ah, Percy, you shall be the first to know. Schmidt will soon be joining us as the butler at Amesworth Court. If he wishes, you may show him some of the house on his way out. Also, would you send Mrs. Howell to me? I need to speak with her. Schmidt, goodbye. I will expect you again very soon."

Her tone was businesslike and authoritative.

It stung that she should dismiss him so easily. He was used to more lingering, regretful farewells from lovely women. The ladies of Estavia—indeed, of most of the courts of Europe—had vied for his attention. And yet he knew that he should accustom himself to such treatment from the countess. This was what a member of the serving class would expect. He was lucky to have a mistress as concerned with her staff as this lady evidently was. His own mother had treated her servants much as she had her children—with casual indifference.

Stifling his annoyance, Michael bowed with just the right amount of deference, then left the room in Percy's wake. The countess had returned already to the papers on her desk.

Chapter Four

*N*early twenty-four hours later, Natalie was still a trifle overset by memories of her own behavior with Schmidt. This was by no means the first time she had indulged in such an unladylike activity as climbing on a desk—in fact, she had been doing it for years. She usually made very sure not to be caught at it, however. That had not happened since Natalie was twelve, shortly after her parents died and she went to live with Aunt Emilia and Uncle James. The scolding Aunt Emilia had delivered on discovering her niece engaged in improper behavior had taught her to be more circumspect, but had not changed her belief that it was usually faster and easier to do something oneself than to depend on servants.

She hadn't meant to be so careless as to allow herself to be discovered on this occasion, either, but she had been busy, and time had gotten away from her. Although she herself had sent word for Michael Schmidt to come at eleven, instructing her staff that he be brought to her directly, she simply had not kept an eye on the clock. Aunt Emilia would have called her a ridiculous hoyden. Heaven only knew what Schmidt had thought of her. Even more disturbing, however, was why she should care what Schmidt thought of her, when he was merely a servant.

When she had agreed to interview a new butler, it never occurred to her to consider what he might look like. She certainly hadn't bargained for a man who exuded intense masculinity. He was at least twenty or thirty years younger than she had expected and devastatingly attractive. Estavia was a German state, she knew, and she had always thought Germans were large and blond and placid. Or perhaps inclined to corpulence and protuberant eyes, as was England's own royal family, which had once been German. Of course, her friend Antonia was small and slim and intense, but she had believed Antonia the exception to the rule.

She had not imagined a dark, lean, hawklike man with gray eyes the color of pale granite and a finely honed body that had seemed, in their one short meeting, poised on the verge of action. In that perilous, heart-stopping moment when she had teetered, arms laden, on the edge of the desk, she had been intensely aware of both the confident speed of his rescue, and the sense of power that emanated from him.

It was difficult for her to concentrate on her duties, but she forced herself to attend to her daily rounds, ending by paying a visit to Alden's cousin Lucretia in that lady's bedchamber. Lucretia Dillerby was nominally Natalie's companion, but, like Max, she fulfilled her duties haphazardly. In Lucretia's case, however, it was not her fault, for she was plagued with a chronic wheezing and shortness of breath. Every late spring and summer she was laid up for weeks at a time.

Returning at last to her boudoir after a chat with Lucretia, Natalie found a sheet of embossed notepaper laid prominently on her escritoire. Apparently Max had finally responded to her urgent request that he provide her with a list of the guests he had invited to "her" house party. Sitting down, she scanned it quickly, then let out a shaky giggle. She had a feeling that "interesting" would be the only ladylike way to describe Max's concept of a suitable guest list.

Lord Anthony Darlington. Mr. Vincent Delamere. Mr. Horace Poricy. Lord Ashford. Mr. John Hamilton. Five young and not-so-young men-about-town. Natalie remembered them from her Seasons in London, although none had been close acquaintances. They were all, however, unmarried, or at least had been when Natalie was last in Town. Since Max mentioned no wives on the list, presumably all remained unwed. Natalie had a strong suspicion that yet another of Max's schemes was unfolding.

Next on the list were Aunt Abbie and Aunt Gracie, Alden's widowed relations, elderly sisters who lived together in a small house outside Maidenhead. Alden had always invited them to Amesworth Court at Christmas and Easter, and Natalie had dutifully continued the tradition after his death. Aunt Abbie was over eighty; Aunt Gracie was still in her seventies but deaf as a stone.

Succeeding them on the guest roster was Mrs. Matilda Raine. Another widow, although considerably younger than Abbie and Gracie. The lady, who admitted to being in her middle forties, was very comfortably endowed, both physically and monetarily. For many years, she'd been Max's acknowledged flirt whenever he was in London.

Then came Viscount and Viscountess Seabury. An inoffensive couple. Viscount Seabury, who must be in his late thirties, was a member of Max's club in London. Emily Lang, now Emily Seabury, had been a pretty blond child without two thoughts to rub together who had come out the same Season as Natalie. Natalie had known her, but the two girls had few interests in common. Since Emily had possessed both a sizable dowry and a strong

desire to marry appropriately, she had been wed by the
end of her first Season.

And, finally, appeared the names of Mr. and Mrs. Raymond Hargrave. Natalie felt a quick stab of pain and put
down the list. She thought she had put her girlhood woes
behind her. Apparently not. Mrs. Raymond Hargrave was
her cousin Jane, with whom she had been raised, and
whom she was presumably supposed to love as a sister.
The two had attended school together and had later
shared a Season. Both had remained unmarried for several years after that, and Jane had been a thorn in Natalie's side as long as they lived together.

Jane had finally married last year. But since Mr. Hargrave was a retiring gentleman with whom Jane had become acquainted while visiting Cheltenham Spa, and the
engagement had been announced a few short weeks after
Alden's death, Natalie had never met him.

Natalie gazed out her window at the park, taking comfort in its serenity. Max truly meant well. Of that she was
convinced. He just couldn't conceive that she had no
wish to resurrect her past life in London.

Alden had understood that. When he proposed to her,
a great deal of the appeal of his offer had been the chance
to gain a home of her own, far away from the misery that
London had come to represent, especially after Giles's
death.

Giles. Natalie's eyes filled with tears. Even now, the
pang that shot through her at the unexpected memory of
her young love was surprisingly painful. She had thought
she had managed to close off that corner of her heart. The
love she had shared with Giles had been a wonderful and
precious emotion, but the pain that had followed the news
of his death had been bitter indeed. Her marriage to
Alden had given her the opportunity to wall that sorrow
away, to build a new life. Now, that life, too, was gone.

With a soft sigh, she dismissed the memories; it did no good to dwell on them. Looking down once more at the list in her hand, she counted again the number of people on it and grimaced. Not only were there significantly more guests than Max had admitted to, but he hadn't managed to even out the numbers. Five unmarried gentlemen, three widowed ladies, and two married couples, added to herself, Lucretia and Max. That made seven ladies and eight gentlemen. They would need another female.

She remembered Max's suggestion of the previous day, that she invite Princess Antonia of Estavia to the house party, and decided crossly that he had most probably realized that his numbers were wrong. Still, the idea of inviting Antonia was most appealing. It might make the house party actually pleasant. With the strain of nursing Alden through his illness and then her period of mourning, it had been years since she had seen any of her girlhood friends.

"I'll do it," she said aloud, causing the housemaid who was coming out of her bedchamber to look at her strangely. But Natalie scarcely noticed her. She reached for a sheet of monogrammed notepaper.

My dearest Antonia, she wrote.

Chapter Five

"*M*ay I speak with your ladyship?"

Natalie restrained herself from jumping at the sound of her new butler's voice behind her. To her ears, even those simple, respectful words seemed to hold a note of masculine appreciation. Such admiration should have been impertinent in a servant, yet she could not make herself take offense. Instead, she felt . . . beautiful. It had been a long time since a young and handsome man had given her that feeling.

And in the three weeks Schmidt had been at Amesworth Court, Natalie had frequently observed that he *was* quite astonishingly handsome—six feet of lean, supple strength, moving with a feral grace that was out of place in a butler. She found it surprising that she had never before noticed how much a butler's plain black silk stockings and severely tailored knee breeches could do for a man's calves. But then, perhaps the man had to have calves like Michael Schmidt's.

She forced herself to turn toward him slowly and calmly. "Yes, Schmidt?"

"Mr. Chesney tells me that soon you will be entertaining a number of distinguished gentlemen, milady."

As it had been ever since he returned from London to take up his position, Schmidt's manner was irreproachable. So why did their conversation somehow seem intimate? She had spoken alone many times with her previous butler and never felt this way.

Unable to help herself, Natalie smiled warmly at the man. "I'm not sure I'd call Max's friends 'distinguished,' Schmidt," she said. This was rather more candor than was strictly appropriate, but something about her butler invited her to speak to him as her equal. "But, yes, we will be entertaining a number of gentlemen from London's *ton*."

Schmidt nodded. "That was the impression Mr. Chesney gave me. I've been assessing the state of your cellars, your ladyship, and I believe some purchases will need to be made."

"Oh?" Natalie raised her eyebrows. "My husband's wine collection was considered exceptional by all discerning critics."

Schmidt seemed untroubled by the implied reproof. "There is no question in my mind as to that, your ladyship. The cellars still hold a number of very fine wines, but it has, if you will excuse me for saying so, clearly been several years since the late earl gave the collection his personal attention."

He turned and looked around the front hall, where they were currently standing. When he had reassured himself that they were not being overheard, he continued. "Not only have some of the older wines gone off, but, according to the cellar record, a significant number of bottles appear to be missing."

"Missing?"

"Is it possible, milady—although I must make it clear that I am only speculating—that some few members of the staff may have been taking advantage of your former lack of a butler."

Natalie looked at him questioningly. "Do you mean

pilfering? Here at Amesworth? What do you think we should do?"

He gave her a serious look in response, his gray gaze level. "I recommend that we do nothing, milady."

"Nothing?"

"If I were to pursue the matter, I could perhaps prove a case against one or two of the footmen and maids. But that would be grounds for dismissal, would it not, milady?"

"Yes . . ." agreed Natalie slowly, "it would."

"Considering the disarray that would ensue from such dismissals, I believe it might be better *not* to pursue the subject directly, your ladyship—not with your house party due to arrive next week."

A stern look appeared on his handsome face. "I have already mentioned—casually, during the servants' dinner hour—that I have just completed an inventory of the cellar stores and that I take pride in my meticulous record keeping. I do not believe any pilfering will happen again, at least as long as I am here."

Natalie considered his statement with approval. Michael Schmidt might be young to be a butler, but he was clearly a man accustomed to command. He would have made a splendid army officer, she thought, if he'd been born to a suitable rank.

Actually, he reminded her more than a little of Giles, who had been serving as a captain under Sir John Moore when he was killed, like his commander, during the terrible retreat on Corunna. Could that resemblance be why she found her new butler so attractive? Perhaps. And yet Michael Schmidt was more than a copy of someone else. He had a power and vibrancy all his own.

Natalie closed her eyes for a moment. For years she had tried to shut away all memories of Giles. Now, thoughts of him seemed to be haunting her. Strangely, though, the pangs she suffered upon remembering him were starting to diminish.

"Is something the matter, milady?"

Natalie snapped out of her brown study. "I'm sorry, Schmidt. I was briefly distracted."

Concern shadowed her butler's pale gray eyes. "I hope you are not feeling ill."

She smiled a trifle wanly. "The last few weeks have been a strain, I must admit. It is never easy to prepare to move houses, and this was not, perhaps, the best time to have guests."

"Maybe you should sit down, milady. I could bring you some tea, or even a little ratafia if you would prefer, in the salon."

Natalie forced herself to laugh. "I'm fine, Schmidt. I don't need tea, and I can't abide ratafia. But you are entirely right about the problem with the wine. I presume you need me to authorize your expenditure on replacements. How much do you think you'll require?"

He named a sum that seemed low to her, compared with the amounts Alden had authorized. She said as much.

"I thought I would take the gig into Bristol, if that met with your approval," he said. "I know a wine importer there who will give me good prices if I deal directly with him."

Natalie couldn't conceal her surprise. "How do you know a merchant in Bristol?"

"A fellow countryman, milady. From Estavia. He'll give me good prices in part because we're countrymen but also because it won't hurt him to be able to say that he supplies the dowager Countess of Amesworth with her wine."

"Oh, yes, I see," murmured Natalie, rather startled. "Clearly you have already thought the matter through quite carefully."

"That is my duty, your ladyship."

"Well, yes, but Stavenger, your predecessor, was content to buy from the same London merchant Amesworth Court has always used. The prices there were far higher." She smiled. "Well, Schmidt, I thank you. For everything. I especially appreciate your efforts to prevent the necessity of dismissing any members of my staff."

He bowed. "Thank you, your ladyship. I will be back from Bristol in time to serve your dinner."

"A long day for you," she said. "It's over fifteen miles to Bristol."

He snapped his fingers. "That's nothing. I've had longer days a hundred times when I was out with—" He broke off.

She looked at him, curious. "Out with . . . ?" she queried.

"Pardon me, milady," he said woodenly, his face blank. "I forgot what I was about to say. Now, if I have your permission, I must be on my way. As you say, it is a distance into Bristol."

He swung around and left without waiting for the permission he had requested. Natalie stood gazing after him as his broad-shouldered back disappeared through the swinging green baize door into the servants' hall. Such an unusual man. She wondered what he had been about to say.

His Highness Prince Michael Rupert Franz Peter von Stell—who was slowly becoming accustomed to being called Schmidt by his employer and Mr. Schmidt by his underlings—sat surveying his private living quarters with some satisfaction. His was a small room high up under the eaves, furnished sparsely with a narrow bed, a chest of drawers, one straight-backed chair, and a washstand holding a basin. A Spartan domain for a prince, perhaps, but the bed was made up with fresh, crisply starched white linen, and the last rays of the evening sun fell cheerfully across the narrow strip of rug on the wooden floor. Through his window, he could see the parkland stretching away toward the home farm. The cows and sheep grazing in the distant meadows lent a sense of rural peace. In all, he found his accommodations a considerable improvement on the dingy lodgings in London he had been forced to take.

Sighing, he kicked his shoes off his tired feet and lay back on the bed. The sun might just be setting, but in July, as it was now, the sunset came at nearly ten o'clock, and he had put in a long day. Driving the gig into Bristol *was* nothing compared to being out on maneuvers with the Estavian army—although he had barely managed to avoid saying so to his pretty little countess. When he had been out on maneuvers, however, he hadn't been required to serve breakfast before and dinner after. Nor had he needed to count all the silver and lock it away before he could retire to his bed.

He lay with one arm over his eyes for a few minutes, then remembered the letter that was still tucked in the pocket of his coat. Josef had passed it to him when he returned from Bristol, but until now Michael had not had a private moment in which to read it. He rolled over on the bed and stretched out one long arm. It was an easy reach across the minuscule room to the chair where his coat hung. Retrieving the letter, he lay back once again and broke the seal. It was from Antonia, of course. He had recognized the handwriting immediately. It was a pity Bath was not on the way to Bristol. It was frustrating to be so close, but he was not due any days off for another two months.

The letter had been written nearly two weeks ago. Of course, he had not told Antonia of his new place of residence, for it would have been difficult to explain to her his new circumstances, so she had directed the letter to his London lodgings. Michael had greased his previous landlord's palm with far more money than he could afford to forward any mail that might arrive for him to Josef. Despite such largesse, however, this letter had clearly sat for a week or more before the man had seen fit to send it on.

He scanned the letter quickly. Apparently Antonia had been invited to a house party by a school friend. Although she called her "my oldest and dearest friend in this country, my darling Nini," she did not mention the friend's last name or where she lived. Michael grinned. That was typical of Antonia. She was always in too great a hurry to waste time on details or formalities.

The name Nini rang a bell with him, however. He remembered Antonia had mentioned her often and with a great deal of fondness during her early days in England. And his sister, for all her little rebellions against unnecessary strictures, had a nice sense of the true proprieties. Therefore, he could trust implicitly that this friend and her house party would be quite unexceptional.

Well, Toni certainly deserved a little gaiety in her life. It was hard on her, mewed up in that academy while she waited for her future to be decided. Of course, it was a princess's duty to marry for the good of her house and country. Carl Friedrich himself had dutifully wed a cold, placid Saxon princess, although he had not seemed to grieve unduly when the girl died after presenting him with the obligatory heir. But this union that Carl Friedrich was setting up for Antonia was another matter altogether.

Michael was increasingly convinced that the emperor of France's star was dimming. The news reaching England of Lord Wellington's advance into Spain this summer was encouraging. Also, Michael, who had visited

Russia some years before, thought that Napoleon was mad to be invading that vast, cold country. So it was not merely his own distaste for the upstart Frenchman that motivated him to thwart Antonia. He did not want his sister's fate tied to that of the House of Bonaparte, as was that of poor Princess Marie Louise of Austria.

Anyway, Michael could not shake the notion that his baby sister was far too young for matrimony. Seventeen might be considered a marriageable age, but it still had been a shock to hear Carl Friedrich's proposal. What could Carl Friedrich be thinking? Michael swore he would do his best to put a stop to the union.

He looked over Toni's letter again. His sister wanted to know whether he thought she should accept the invitation or whether she should stay at school, as Carl Friedrich had directed. Michael laughed. It would undoubtedly drive Carl Friedrich to distraction to hear that Antonia was jaunting around England, but why shouldn't she have a little fun? He would write tonight and suggest that she accept the invitation.

Chapter Six

"Schmidt?"

Michael jumped at the sound of the countess's low, throaty voice directly behind him. Pricking his finger on the rose that he had been adjusting minutely in its arrangement, he knocked the bloom to the floor.

"Darn," he muttered under his breath, knowing full well that a well-trained butler would never allow such evidence of emotion to show. Nor would he ever swear in the presence of his superiors, especially a lady. Hastily, he kneeled to retrieve the fallen flower.

He found himself face to face with a pair of slender ankles, enticingly clad in sheer silk stockings above delicate black kid slippers.

This is not going well, he thought savagely. It was certainly difficult to be a proper servant when one's employer was this pretty.

He stood slowly, trying not to look at the countess, but that was impossible. She had recently elected to celebrate the warm weather and her emergence from mourning by donning a series of light summer muslins that clung to her slender figure.

"The flowers look lovely there," Natalie said, gesturing at the arrangement on the ormolu table in the center of the entrance hall. The pale green Chinese porcelain bowl, filled with a riot of red, pink, and yellow roses, warmed the black-and-white marble-floored room beautifully.

"Thank you, milady," Michael said without expression, striving to appear more like a butler than he had yet managed to achieve in this particular encounter. "I consider it creates a nice effect."

Natalie smiled at him, a dimple flickering in her left cheek. Did she have any idea what that dimple did to him? Of course she didn't. She thought him a servant, not a man.

"It's just right," she said. "How are you and the staff managing, Mr. Schmidt? Are you ready for our first guests to arrive?"

"Yes, your ladyship. All the rooms are prepared, and Cook has already begun dinner for fourteen. There is also a cold collation set out in the gold parlor for any guests who arrive early and wish a small meal."

"That sounds perfect. Thank you, Schmidt." She looked down at the letter she was holding. "I apologize for inconveniencing the staff at this late date, but one additional guest will be arriving tomorrow. My dearest friend from school has just written to say that she would love to come. She is sorry to reply so late, but she wanted to ask her brother's opinion before responding, and I gather he was away from home. I suppose that, what with the war, it takes a while to write to Germany."

A foreboding chill ran through Michael.

"I have suddenly realized," said Natalie, "that you must be acquainted with my guest. I am referring to Princess Antonia of Estavia."

A most unprofessional, gargling choke escaped Michael's lips.

Natalie turned an inquiring eye upon him as he struggled to control himself. When he continued to cough, her expression became one of concern. "Are you all right?" she asked. "Is something the matter?"

"I'm sorry, your ladyship," he said when he could speak again. "I am inclined to think I must have inhaled a small gnat. I do apologize."

She smiled warmly. "These unfortunate things do happen. I am sorry to see you in such discomfort."

"I am fine," he said stiffly, while his mind raced. Antonia, arriving the next day. She would undoubtedly blurt out that he was her brother. Even if, by some miracle, he managed to avoid that particular pitfall, he still faced the problem of explaining to Toni what he was doing serving as a butler.

Josef was ironing cravats when Michael tracked him down. He smiled when he saw his master. "We haven't been able to talk much lately, my—"

Michael frowned.

"We haven't been able to talk much lately . . . Michael," Josef amended.

Michael closed the door behind himself. "We may be alone now, Josef, but if you don't call me Michael in private as well as when we are with others, you're going to make a mistake one day."

Josef dipped another cravat in starch, then lifted a hot iron off the fire and applied it with meticulous care to the fabric. "Mr. Chesney is very particular about his cravats," he said, avoiding the subject at hand. "He won't allow the laundry maid to iron them. Says she leaves creases."

Michael perched on the windowsill. Then he smiled. "This reminds me of when I was a little boy. Do you remember that you washed and ironed and mended my clothes yourself, because the housekeeper would tattle to my mother if too many sets of clothes were sent to the laundry?"

"Princess Elise was very particular in her require-ments," said Josef diplomatically.

"My mother was a cold prig," Michael said. "She felt I should endlessly study my lessons and attend state func-tions dressed to perfection. Thank heaven that when I fi-nally grew old enough for 'manly' pursuits, my father saw to it that I hunted and fished and drilled with the army. And thank heavens for you, Josef."

Michael lapsed into silence, and Josef continued iron-ing.

After several minutes of quiet companionship, Michael spoke again. "The countess has just informed me that Toni will be arriving at Amesworth Court tomorrow," he said casually.

Josef laid down the iron and stared at Michael. "Princess Antonia? Coming here?"

Michael nodded. "Yes. Princess Antonia has been in-vited as part of the house party." He laughed. "I told you that I'd recently encouraged Toni to visit her old friend Nini. Well, I guess now we know who Nini is."

"B-b-but . . . b-but . . ." Josef stuttered.

Michael nodded again. "You sum up my sentiments exactly, Josef."

A sudden strong scent of scorching filled the room. Josef whipped the iron off the cravat upon which it was resting and looked down guiltily at the triangular brown imprint in its center.

Placing the iron back against the fire, Josef sighed, then shrugged. "Mr. Chesney has no idea how many cra-vats he owns. He won't miss one," he said.

Michael picked up the mistreated cravat and stuffed it into his pocket. "I will dispose of the evidence."

"Do you have any other startling revelations?" Josef asked acerbically. "If so, I think I must shift my efforts to something less potentially destructive." Picking up a pair of Max Chesney's pantaloons, he produced a brush and started energetically removing the mud spattered on their lower portions.

After a few minutes, he looked up. "What do you intend to do about your sister?" he asked. "I am merely inquiring, you understand."

Michael, who had sat down on the windowsill once again, shrugged. "To be honest, I haven't the slightest idea."

Josef looked him over. "I suppose there is no point in suggesting that you take this opportunity posthaste to leave a profession so unsuited to your rank?"

"Absolutely none," Michael said firmly.

"It's the only solution I can see."

"I'd have to leave today—without giving any sort of notice. I can't do that."

"I don't see why not," Josef argued. "You shan't need a reference."

"Even putting aside the fact that leaving a position without notice is unethical behavior, unsuitable to a von Stell of Estavia, I couldn't possibly desert the countess at such a time. What would she do about her house party?"

"Aaaahh . . ." said Josef.

Michael glared. "And what exactly does 'Ah' mean?" he asked.

Josef raised innocent eyes. "Why, nothing." He returned to his brushing.

Michael tapped the windowsill impatiently. "I know it meant something," he said. "Your voice always gets that tone when you remember that you used to wash my dirty hands and wipe my snotty nose."

"It meant nothing." Josef applied himself even more vigorously to his brushing. "Except . . ."

"Except what?"

"You seem to have gotten rather attached to this household . . ."

"I said I would do a job, and I will do it."

". . . and to its mistress?" Josef added in an inquiring tone.

Michael flushed. "Josef, I very kindly refrained from throwing you out a window when I discovered how you had misled me concerning the lady. What are you hinting at now?"

Josef turned away. "Nothing, nothing," he said hastily.

"If I were you, then," Michael warned, "I would keep my mouth shut."

Josef bowed. "As your highness commands. And what, exactly, does your highness intend to do about Princess Antonia?"

Michael gave him a black scowl. "Please remember to call me Michael, and I have no idea. Perhaps one will come to me."

Josef snorted. "I wish you luck . . . Michael."

Michael jumped down from the sill. "You're no help. I don't know why I bother to tell you at all."

"Because you value my opinion?" Josef suggested.

Michael stalked to the door. "If you ever do come up with a useful opinion, please let me know. But I'm not going to sneak away from Amesworth Court like a thief in the dark, so you can put that notion out of your head."

He left without looking back, so he missed Josef's small, triumphant smile. In that loyal retainer's humble opinion, his royal highness was considerably more enamored of the countess than he yet realized.

Chapter Seven

*N*atalie smiled as her personal maid, Gwyneth, adjusted the pier glass so Natalie could see her reflection.

"Yes, I think that should do nicely," she said, looking at herself in the pale green silk crepe evening dress trimmed with silver ribbons. Gwyneth had threaded matching silver ribbons through her mistress's hair. Even though the gown was three years out of date, Natalie felt the effect remained elegant, and this dress had been Alden's favorite.

Picking up a silk shawl fashioned in a slightly deeper green embroidered with silver, she allowed her maid to drape it about her shoulders. "Thank you, Gwyneth," she said. "It's after seven. I must go downstairs now. I'm afraid some of the guests may already have gathered."

Reaching the ground floor, she signaled to Percy, who was waiting beside the door to the blue drawing room, to keep it closed while she paused to collect herself. Amesworth Court had been her home for three years, but in that time it had been empty of all but her, Alden, his cousins, and the servants. The buzz of voices was new, and she was not completely sure she liked it. But, whether or not she did, she had to face it. These were her guests. She nodded to Percy to open the door.

She was a few minutes late but not intolerably so. Only a few of the guests had gathered before her arrival. Natalie moved to the pale blue silk sofa on which Emily Seabury was seated alone.

"Emily," she said, settling next to the young blond woman and preparing to be a congenial hostess. "We didn't have much time to talk when you arrived earlier, and it's been such an age since we've seen each other. I hope your room is comfortable."

Lady Seabury smiled politely. "Oh, yes, thank you, Natalie. It's very pleasant. And what a lovely room this one is. Of course, I'm sure you know I've never been to Amesworth before."

Natalie allowed her gaze to dwell fondly on the ice blue silk walls that matched the upholstery of the gilt furniture, and then on the cream and white decorative plasterwork on the ceiling. "I'm especially fond of this room. Alden's grandmother decorated it, and I think it does reveal a certain feminine touch, don't you agree?"

Before Emily could reply, the door opened and Lucretia hurried in, her shawl slightly askew.

"My dear Natalie," she panted, hastening across the room. "I apologize for being late. I had no idea of the time."

"That's quite all right, Lucretia," Natalie said soothingly. "Emily, I don't recall that you have met Alden's cousin, Miss Dillerby. Lucretia, this is Lady Seabury. I am counting on you to make her feel at home here. I must speak with some of my other guests."

She rose and walked through the room, chatting quietly with each of the visitors. She had barely spoken more than a few words with Max and his London flirt, Matilda Raine, who were sitting comfortably together on a sofa near the door, when she heard a peevish voice from outside the room.

"Don't just stand there gaping, my man. Pick up my reticule."

Natalie tensed. It was hard to believe that after several years the mere sound of Jane's voice could still upset her, but there it was. Even at the age of twelve, when Natalie had first gone to live with the Thorpes, she had not gotten along with Cousin Jane.

The door opened, and Jane, now Mrs. Raymond Hargrave, appeared in the entrance, accompanied by a man who had to be her husband. Natalie regarded her with an unreasonable but familiar annoyance. Why, she wondered crossly, did Jane, after so many years of complaining about Natalie's manner of dressing, continue to display so little clothes sense? During their shared debutante years, the whites and pale pinks and blues considered suitable for their age had looked terrible with Jane's sallow skin, and she had openly and often criticized Natalie, who looked much better in them. But surely now Jane could seize the opportunities offered a married woman to wear something more becoming. Natalie would have picked a deep plum for her, or perhaps a bright cherry. Almost anything other than the amber gown in which she was clad. No matter how fashionable a color it might be, it did nothing for Jane's dull brown hair and eyes.

Forcing a smile to her lips, Natalie moved forward. "Jane, how lovely that you finally made it to Amesworth Court after all this time. I'm so sorry that I was dressing when you arrived. I do hope my staff made you comfortable."

"I suppose so," Jane said. "Although the water in my pitcher was not as hot as I would like it. And I'm surprised you didn't make an effort to greet your cousin yourself."

Natalie kept her smile fixed. How like Jane to greet

her with complaints. "I'm sorry to hear about your water. I'll see that the maid is properly instructed as to your preferences."

She turned to the man standing beside her cousin. "You must be my new cousin-in-law, Mr. Hargrave. I'm sorry I could not attend your wedding, but I'm sure you knew I was in mourning."

She held out a hand and he took it.

"Of course, no one would expect a recent widow to indulge in social intercourse," he said in a pompous tone. "My mother has remained withdrawn ever since the death of my father twenty years ago." He eyed Natalie's green dress and its silver ribbons with a hint of disapproval, as if he had expected her to be in mourning still.

"Allow me to introduce you to some of the other gentlemen," Natalie said hastily. She led the way to a small knot of elegantly attired guests. "Lord Seabury, Lord Anthony, Mr. Hamilton, do you know my cousin's husband, Mr. Hargrave?"

"I have not had the pleasure," Lord Seabury said politely, and the other two murmured their agreement.

"I live retired in Gloucestershire, occupied with my studies," said Mr. Hargrave. "I am cataloguing the mushrooms of England."

The three other gentlemen blinked. Clearly, none of them had ever considered mushrooms in any form other than on a plate.

"I'm sure you will find plenty to discuss," said Natalie, retiring hurriedly.

That, of course, left her with Jane. Perhaps she would have done better to discuss fungi.

"Jane," she said, "come sit with me. How are you? Does marriage suit you?"

"I am very well indeed," Jane replied. "It is a great pleasure to live with a man of such intellect as Raymond.

There are few to match him. But, Natalie, I have never had a chance to give you in person my condolences on your husband's death. It must be so sad for you that your life has ended before it has barely begun."

Everything Jane said was always so proper, Natalie thought bitterly, that she could not reasonably object. Yet each word her cousin uttered managed to set her teeth on edge.

"I am very happy here," she said quietly.

"But you cannot help but wish now that you had chosen more wisely," Jane insisted. "Of course, you are older than I, so I can see that you felt forced to accept your first offer. But to marry a man so much older than yourself . . . You must regret it now."

Natalie clenched her hands in her lap. She was only six weeks older than Jane, and the rest of Jane's statement was unfairly inaccurate. She had turned down proposals from a number of eligible *partis* in favor of Giles. To her knowledge, no man other than Raymond Hargrave had been willing to overlook Jane's plain appearance and sharp tongue. These trivial concerns should not have mattered in the least, but Jane brought out the worst in her.

"Alden was just past fifty, and your husband must be at least forty," she heard herself say waspishly, in a way quite unlike herself. She cast a look at Mr. Hargrave, assessing his receding, mousy hair and stooped shoulders. *And he is not one-tenth as handsome as Alden was, either, and forty is probably a kindness*, she added silently.

Jane followed her gaze. "Dear Raymond. He was so pleased when I consented to wed him. He calls me his muse."

"For his mushroom catalogue?" Natalie asked, astonishment overcoming any thought of good manners.

"Raymond's catalogue is a very important work," Jane said chillingly. "But, Natalie, we were so surprised to be invited to this house party. I quite thought you would still be in mourning. But now that I see the gentlemen you have invited, I understand your reasons. You have no wish to remain a widow. Of course, you must make your own choice, but if my Raymond died, I know I would never have the heart . . ." She let her words trail off, her disapproval obvious if unspoken.

"Excuse me," Natalie said. "I have recollected a detail I must attend to regarding dinner. I shall return directly."

Before Jane could protest, she hurried out of the room, gesturing to Percy to close the door behind her. She needed a few minutes of privacy to collect herself.

She walked through several antechambers to the front hall, where she was far beyond Percy's sight. Sinking down onto the marble staircase, she rested her head on her hand. If she hadn't left the room, she thought she might have slapped Jane and that would never do. She hadn't slapped Jane since she was thirteen. As she remembered, at the time Jane had said something slighting about French emigrées. Since Natalie's beloved mother had been French, and Jane clearly meant to include her in the remark, Natalie had been unable to restrain herself. That lack of control gained her a birching from Uncle James and two days of confinement in her room. After that, she had learned to keep her feelings to herself.

She clenched her free hand tightly. She had escaped the Thorpe family and its miserable memories. Why had Max insisted on inviting Jane to this ridiculous house party?

"Your ladyship," said a deep, startled voice. "Are you unwell?"

Natalie looked up to see Michael Schmidt standing in front of her, concern on his handsome face.

"No, no, I'm fine," she said. She knew she should rise from the step, but she was unwilling to move. The black, painful anger Jane had aroused in her still overwhelmed her.

Michael regarded her intently for a moment, then sank down on the step beside her. He placed a large, gentle hand atop hers.

"Your hands are like ice," he said. "Are you sure you are not ill?"

She struggled to find something decorous to say. "I— I was upset by a remark my cousin made to me," she blurted.

He said nothing but took her hands in both of his and gently warmed them. Such an intimacy was incredibly improper, yet she didn't withdraw from his grasp. Despite the gentleness of his touch, she could feel the steel in his grip that lay just beneath the surface.

She wondered why she was confiding her private affairs to her butler, yet spoke further. "My cousin Jane. I was brought up with her, but we were never friends."

Michael released her hands and stood. "I know something of unhappy families," he said finally. "I am sorry that you should suffer so."

At his kind words, she felt ready to rise herself. She even forced a smile. "I wouldn't call it suffering," she said, taking the hand he offered and allowing him to help her stand. "I was merely stung by a silly childish spat that has continued into adulthood."

He stood beside her, his fingers still cradling hers, his concerned gray eyes revealing that he did not believe her easy disclaimer.

She disengaged her hand to rearrange her shawl, distancing herself from him mentally as well as physically. "Is dinner ready, Schmidt?" she asked formally.

"Yes, your ladyship," he replied, immediately following her lead and becoming the perfect butler once again.

"I think we should serve it now. Please tell the kitchen," she said."I will return to my guests."

"Yes, your ladyship."

She stepped further away from him, moving toward the blue drawing room and her guests, but she knew that he did not immediately follow her order. Rather, she could sense him standing motionless at the foot of the steps, watching her with his penetrating gray eyes as she walked across the hall.

Chapter Eight

$\mathcal{A}$t eleven of the clock the next morning, Michael was still unable to decide what he would do when his sister arrived. He could scarcely avoid welcoming Princess Antonia to Amesworth Court; his professional duties required it. Perhaps fortune would smile on him, and he would have a few moments alone with her to explain the situation. Although exactly *how* he was going to explain it, still eluded him.

Adding to his discomfort was his recollection of his exchange with the countess the evening before. Such intimate behavior was totally impermissible in a servant. But when he had seen Natalie sitting pathetically on the stairs, and when she had looked up at him with her big blue eyes, he had been unable to control himself.

He sighed and turned to Percy, who was on duty by the front door. Instantly, his ruminations were halted at a shocking sight.

"My lord, man, what has happened to your gloves?" he asked in horror.

Percy looked down with a perplexed frown at his white gloves, which were smudged with soot.

"I'm not sure," he said. Then he brightened. "Oh! I know. Betty was carrying the coal scuttle to the morning room, and it was much too heavy for her. There must have been soot on the handle."

Michael hid a grin. Betty was the newest maid, hired just the previous week because of the house party. A local farmer's daughter, she was a stalwart lass capable of handling a load far heavier than a coal scuttle. It had been apparent from the start that Percy was smitten with her. That was no excuse, however, for the condition of his gloves.

"Were you planning to open the door with your gloves in that condition?" Michael asked sternly. "We are expecting both Mr. Delamere and Princess Antonia of Estavia to arrive momentarily."

"A princess," Percy said, struck. "Wouldn't do to greet her with dirty gloves."

Michael sighed. Percy was a local boy, too, hired on to the staff after the old earl fell ill. He was a well-meaning lad but still a trifle bucolic.

"It would not do to greet any of her ladyship's guests with dirty gloves," he corrected. "Now, go and change them immediately. I hope you have clean ones."

"I think I do."

"If you don't, you'll have to borrow a pair from Oliver. And in future make sure you always have clean ones of your own."

"Yes, Mr. Schmidt," Percy said. It had not taken him long to realize that, while the new butler might be foreign, he was not to be trifled with. A sharp eye he had— and a sharp tongue when things were not performed to his exacting standards.

"I'll take your post by the door," Michael said. "But do hurry. I do not wish the countess to discover you away from your post." He sat down in the chair by the front door.

Moments later, however, Natalie came flying down the stairs, her cheeks flushed a delicate pink, her blue-

gray eyes wide with excitement. She was wearing a white
muslin morning dress, cut with a high ruffle at the collar
and trimmed with rose-colored ribbons. Despite the
gown's demure neckline and virginal style, she looked
entrancing.

"Open the door, Schmidt!" she cried as she ran down
the last few steps, "Princess Antonia is coming! I just saw
the carriage enter the park." In her enthusiasm, she failed
to notice the missing Percy.

Michael opened the door, and Natalie instantly darted
onto the wide front steps. He followed her, more sedately.

The coach from Amesworth that Natalie had sent to
transport Toni was indeed rounding the ornamental lake
at a brisk trot. But as Michael and Natalie watched, a
sporting high-perch phaeton, drawn by a pair of spirited
chestnuts, came bowling up the drive behind it.

The driver, a young buck with a great many capes to
his driving coat, made no effort to slacken his pace to ac-
commodate that of the slower carriage, but rather pulled
around it at a fast canter. As he did so, however, one
wheel of his phaeton locked with the rear wheel on the
Amesworth coach. The coach wobbled, then teetered toward the lake.

Natalie gasped.

Michael let loose a string of pungent curses in German.

The driver of the phaeton jerked his reins, pulling his
wheel free at the last moment. Guiding his horses onto
the mown parkland, he regained the drive in front of the
Amesworth coach. The coachman, a venerable driver of
many years' service, soothed his startled horses and
safely regained the roadway himself.

The young buck looked back. Seeing that he had not
overset the carriage, he gave a cheery wave and continued up the drive.

"Damned idiot," Michael muttered under his breath,

too overcome by emotion to remain properly impassive or discreet.

Natalie turned at his remark, and Michael stared stonily ahead, ready for her condemnation.

Instead, she grinned. "I quite agree, Schmidt. That was a ridiculous piece of foolish bravado. I see that Mr. Delamere has not gained any common sense since I was last in London."

With a spurt of gravel, Mr. Delamere's phaeton halted at the foot of the steps. His tiger jumped down and scurried to the horses' heads.

Mr. Delamere waved at Natalie. "Lady Amesworth, how kind of you to invite me!" he called cheerfully, as if the incident in the drive had not occurred.

"You are most welcome," she said tightly.

The Amesworth carriage pulled up behind the phaeton. The groom riding behind hastened to let down the steps. Antonia was already peering out.

"Nini!" she called, "Nini!" She waved to her friend.

Mr. Delamere turned around and spotted Toni. His eyes widened in appreciation.

Michael followed the direction of his gaze and gritted his teeth. Toni was a beautiful child, and she looked particularly lovely today. She seemed to have grown more mature in the weeks since they had last been together. Her gown was simple, but it showed off her petite form, and she had released her braids into stylish curls.

Mr. Delamere clearly approved of what he saw. Hurrying to the Amesworth carriage, he offered Toni his arm. "My dear young lady, allow me to assist you," he said.

Antonia flashed him a merry smile. Placing her hand on his arm, she danced down the steps.

"Vincent Delamere, at your service," said Mr. Delamere, his gaze roaming approvingly over Antonia's dainty form. He smiled and took her hand in his. "How delightful that this house party will be graced with such beauty."

Michael ground his teeth.

Antonia laughed and peered up at her courtier through long dark eyelashes. Quite obviously, she had an instinctive understanding of flirtation. "I'm Antonia von Stell. I thought we were going to be pitched into the lake."

"Miss von Stell, how wonderful to meet you. I'm sorry your coachman was so clumsy, but I'm glad I was able to prevent an accident. I am a notable whip, you know."

Antonia fluttered her lashes demurely and sent Vincent Delamere an admiring glance.

Michael had to restrain himself from bolting down the steps and forcibly parting the two. Delamere was a brash young cockerel whose arrogant self-esteem was the size of Westminster Abbey, but Antonia was far too innocent and unsophisticated to realize it. Michael admitted that the handsome young man did show off to advantage in his tight buckskins and lavish driving coat.

He'd missed Antonia's reply, but she was laughing again. Delamere had not yet released her hand, but she didn't seem to mind.

In another moment, Michael knew that he was going to sacrifice his job by knocking this young man to the ground.

"My dear Antonia," said Natalie, who had walked down the outside steps during this interchange and approached Toni.

Antonia turned and squealed in excitement. She had been achieving a fine approximation of sophistication, but now she reverted to the child Michael was more familiar with.

"Nini, darling Nini!" she cried. "It's been an age! Oh, how perfect to see you again." She threw her arms around Natalie, Vincent Delamere completely forgotten.

Michael was pleased to see that Mr. Delamere looked distinctly put out.

"Nini!" Antonia squealed again. "You haven't changed a mite. I can't believe it."

Natalie held her at arm's length. "You, on the other hand, have grown up. Why, I barely recognize you, so stylish you're looking. Oh, my dearest, it is wonderful to see you again. We will have so much to talk about. Letters can only say so much. Come inside with me and I will see you settled." She wrapped her arm around Antonia's waist to guide her up the steps.

Since Percy still had not returned, Michael moved to hold open the door for them.

Halfway up the stairs, Natalie guiltily remembered her other guest. Mr. Delamere was standing in the driveway, a sulky pout on his face.

"Please excuse me for a moment, Toni," she said, and she turned back down the stairs. "My dear Mr. Delamere," she said, "you must forgive me. I didn't mean to ignore you, but I haven't seen my dear school friend in years, and the excitement quite overcame me. I do apologize for my neglect. How charming to see you again. Welcome to Amesworth Court. Please, do come inside."

Antonia, meanwhile, left halfway up the steps, had moved to the top. There, she came face to face with Michael, standing at the door.

"Michael!" she gasped under her breath, clearly—and fortunately—too shocked to say anymore.

The moment of truth had arrived, Michael realized, and with Natalie still engaged with Delamere, they had a modicum of privacy.

Michael placed one finger to his lips. "Don't say anything," he whispered.

"Michael," Antonia whispered back, "whatever are you doing here?"

"Shh. I'll explain later," he muttered. "For now, just ignore me."

"Ignore you?" she gasped.

"Antonia, for the love of God, please be quiet," he hissed.

"Wh—"

"Don't say anything. Anything at all. To anyone."

"But—"

"Toni . . ."

Vincent Delamere and his hostess were now halfway up the steps, she listening attentively to his discourse. Michael stiffened his back against the door and gazed straight ahead, pointedly ignoring his sister.

Antonia stared at him wide-eyed, but finally turned back to her friend.

Michael almost sagged in relief.

But he still had no idea what his next move would be. Except for one thing. He was going to creep into Vincent Delamere's room some night soon and wring the wretched dandy's neck.

Chapter Nine

*T*o Michael's relief, Antonia had no further chance to
speak with him, for Natalie immediately swept her
upstairs to her private apartments. Vincent Delamere was
left, looking rather aggrieved, to be escorted upstairs by
Percy, who had reappeared with a fresh pair of gloves.
Michael knew the source of Delamere's annoyance. Natalie had not been inhospitable in any way to the
wretched dandy, but she had inadvertently made it clear
that he was not the center of her attention. And Delamere
was accustomed to considering himself the focal point of
all feminine eyes.

Feeling rather grumpy himself, Michael went to the
butler's pantry below stairs, where he commenced the
herculean task of removing the necessary silver for that
night's dinner from the silver safe. Piece by piece, he
counted the flatware, the serving platters and bowls, the
huge branched candelabra, and the two ornamental
epergnes, setting to one side anything that the footmen
would need to polish. At least it had been gratifying to
see how much Natalie cared for his young sister, he
mused. Upon reflection, he didn't think he had ever seen
Natalie as relaxed and cheerful. Had he ever heard her
giggle like a schoolgirl before? It had been a charming
sound.

"Michael!" hissed an instantly recognizable voice from the hallway.

He jumped, dropping a serving fork, which clattered to the stone flags.

"Michael," came the low whisper again. "Whatever are you doing here?"

Leaving the fork at his feet, Michael slowly turned to find Antonia peering round the doorframe in an attitude of extreme secrecy.

Michael couldn't help smiting himself on the forehead, although the gesture was as melodramatic as any of Antonia's. Somehow, his little sister seemed singularly successful at generating melodrama. He hastened to the door, grabbed Toni by the shoulders, pulled her into the butler's pantry, then checked the corridor outside. To his relief, it was empty, though the sound of voices floated clearly down the hall from the kitchen.

"Did anyone see you coming here?" he demanded.

Antonia raised innocent sea green eyes to his. "Oh, no, Michael. I was very, very careful. I tiptoed all the way."

Michael shut the door. "In that case," he said crossly, "anyone who saw you would immediately wonder what you were up to."

"But I just told you, dearest, nobody did see me," Antonia explained earnestly.

"I am most relieved."

"But that's what I wanted to ask you about, Michael," Antonia said. She looked around the butler's pantry with a puzzled air. "Why shouldn't anyone see me? And what are *you* doing here?"

Michael sighed. He had known he couldn't avoid this question forever.

"I didn't ask Nini, Michael dear, because I could see you did not want me to do so, but I have been racking and racking my brains for the answer. What are you doing here in Nini's home, when she does not seem to know who you are?"

"Well . . ." Michael searched desperately for a reasonable explanation. If he told Toni the truth, she would immediately insist on joining him as a scullery maid, and that was inconceivable.

"I thought and thought while I was talking with Nini," Antonia continued, "and suddenly I realized what the truth must be. Of course, it was obvious once I thought of it."

Michael stared at her. "It is?" he asked suspiciously.

Antonia pulled his head down and whispered portentously in his ear. "I have realized that, of course, you are here spying, Michael."

Michael's jaw dropped. *Spying* was an excuse he had never—even at his most desperate—considered.

"Well, that had to be it. I see that now," Antonia continued blithely. "Why else would a prince be posing as a butler?"

"Umm . . . well . . . yes," Michael muttered.

"Now, Michael, I am sure that you are forbidden to speak of your mission, so I won't nag at you to tell me more. But I did want you to know that I knew."

"Yes . . . um . . . yes. I appreciate that, Toni." With an effort, Michael attempted to hide his disbelief. He could not imagine who on earth Toni possibly thought he might be spying on here at Amesworth Court. Or for whom, for that matter. Still, her absurd conclusion seemed a heaven-sent solution to his dilemma. If Toni believed he was here on some secret mission, she would be willing to accept his lowly position as a servant without a fuss.

Relieved, he gave her a giant if belated embrace. "What a clever child you are, Toni," he said. "How like you to have worked it out like that. But I know I can rely on your absolute silence on the subject." There, he thought proudly, he hadn't actually told a single lie.

Antonia beamed. "Oh, Michael, darling," she said, "I would never, ever betray you. But surely there is something I could do to help you in your objective."

Michael kissed her cheek. "Toni, my dear, your task must be to ignore me totally. I know it's a difficult effort I'm asking of you, but I am confident of your abilities."

Antonia pouted. "Oh, Michael, but I . . ."

Michael assumed his big brother voice. "Absolutely not, Toni. I cannot allow you to expose yourself to any . . . danger—" he improvised. Too late, he realized the trap into which he had fallen. Antonia would likely find the thought of danger deliciously romantic. He attempted to recover. "Antonia, sweetheart, it is very, very important that you remain in ignorance of my role here. Do you think you can manage that?"

Antonia was crestfallen. "I suppose so, Michael. But it doesn't sound as if it will be as much fun."

"It is your duty, Antonia," Michael said firmly, summoning up the voice of their Prussian mother.

Automatically, Antonia responded. "I suppose so, Michael. But if there's anything else I can do, you will tell me, won't you?"

Michael squeezed her shoulder and released her. "Of course, my darling. But you really must run along now. It would be bad for . . . my mission if anyone were to see you here."

"Yes, yes," Antonia agreed. "I am being very careful. On my way down, I did tiptoe all the way."

"Good," said Michael, giving her another quick kiss. "Now, run along, *liebchen*."

And with one wistful backward glance, Antonia did exactly that.

Michael sighed. What an improbable manner in which to have his dilemma solved—providing, of course, that his imaginative and impetuous little sister did not attempt to involve herself in this "secret mission."

"I picked up a very fine hunter at Tat's just last week. A beautiful bay. One of Lord Dinsdorf's," remarked Lord Anthony Darlington, who was seated on Natalie's right.

Viscount Seabury, seated on her left, was not quite so rude as to lean across his hostess, but his interest in horseflesh betrayed him into talking across her.

"Oh, really," he said. "Dinsdorf is selling off some of his horses? I hadn't heard that. You're a lucky dog, Darlington, if that's the bay I'm thinking of. I had my eye on it all last season. You should have seen it take a huge hedge and ditch down in the Shires in January. One clean bound . . ."

Natalie sighed. Darlington and Seabury had been discussing sporting events all evening. Occasionally they would remember their hostess and attempt to include her in the conversation, but within moments they would be off again, nattering endlessly about hunting or horses or hounds. She had no interest in the subject and less to add. She enjoyed horses herself and even the occasional local hunt, but she had never ridden to hounds in the Shires and certainly had no acquaintance with pugilism, the other topic her dinner companions pursued relentlessly.

Deciding that her only recourse was to ignore the gentlemen on either side of her, she attempted to hear what else was being discussed at her dinner table.

"The *Oudemnsiella mucida* is considered by many to be a very beautiful example of a mushroom, but I myself prefer the *Calocera viscosa*," Raymond Hargrave was droning to Emily Seabury, who looked positively green with boredom. Natalie sighed in sympathy for poor Emily before turning her attention to another conversation.

"And our esteemed Secretary for War—Lord

Castlereagh—told me specifically that the government has not as yet made up its mind on that point," intoned Mr. Horace Poricy self-importantly. "Of course, when they do, I will be one of the first to know."

Natalie questioned that. Mr. Poricy's post in the government was not nearly as important as he liked to imply. He was indeed a secretary at the War Office, but a relatively junior one considering his years of service. She remembered Alden commenting bluntly, after they had encountered Poricy at a London party, that he doubted Poricy had ever had a confidential conversation with a senior government minister in his life, despite Poricy's constant inflated claims to the contrary.

"What, what was that?" bellowed Aunt Gracie, raising her ear trumpet. "Speak up, young man! So typical of your generation to mumble into your soup."

Mr. Poricy, who was on the shady side of fifty, flushed red, and turned away to Natalie's cousin Jane, on his left. Natalie silently wished Jane well with the conversation. They deserved each other, since Mr. Poricy was as smug as Jane was overbearing.

Honestly, thought Natalie crossly, Max must have oatmeal for brains. What was he thinking to have invited this lot?

She glanced farther down the table. The only person who seemed to be enjoying herself at all was young Antonia von Stell, who was conversing animatedly with Vincent Delamere. Watching the seventeen-year-old lean closer to her dinner companion in order to shake a finger at him reprovingly, Natalie noticed once again how much the girl was growing up. Vincent Delamere would bear watching, however, since his appreciation for his dinner partner's youthful curves was more obvious than Natalie liked.

"May I offer you anything further, sir?" asked Michael

Schmidt, suddenly appearing between the conversing couple.

Vincent Delamere looked up in annoyance, and Natalie wondered at her normally suave butler's gauche interruption of the conversation.

"No, thank you," Delamere said brusquely. "I have plenty already."

"But no potatoes," said Michael firmly. "Here, let me serve you."

His usually dexterous movements were clumsy, however, and several of the cream-colored balls, shiny with butter and coated in parsley, rolled from the silver serving platter directly into Delamere's lap.

Delamere shot up from his chair, shouting, "You oaf!"

Unfortunately, this action only called the attention of the entire table to his predicament. He flushed beetroot red as he realized what a ridiculous sight he made with a greasy trail of butter and parsley down the front of his primrose-colored superfine evening breeches.

Stuttering with rage, he left the room hurriedly.

"I'll have words with your mistress about this," he said darkly from the door to Michael. "For now, you can send my valet to me immediately."

Natalie fought an impulse to put her head down on the table, though whether she would then succumb to laughter or tears she was not quite sure. Of one thing was she certain: this house party Max had contrived would be the worst social event of her life.

"What's this I hear about the imperturbable Michael Schmidt behaving less than impeccably at dinner?" asked Josef, who was sitting with his feet up on the table in the butler's pantry, a mug of stout in his hand.

Michael closed the door to the hallway. "Heard the gossip, have you?"

"Most of it, I should think," said Josef serenely. "Delamere's valet is ranting in the laundry room over the ruination of a new pair of breeches. Percy and Oliver are giggling in the footmen's room because they've never seen you make a mistake. They stopped as soon as I came in, but I'd heard enough. I gather Mr. Delamere was sitting next to Princess Antonia."

"He damn near had his hand in her lap," Michael growled.

Josef arched his eyebrows.

"Well, it was certainly very close to her lap," Michael amended. "I suppose he might really have been rescuing his napkin."

"How did Princess Antonia react to this behavior?" Josef inquired mildly.

"Princess Antonia," Michael said with emphasis, "is a foolish young girl who thinks she has turned into an adult overnight."

"Well, she *is* seventeen now, my prince. Your brother believes her old enough to be betrothed."

"My brother is a fool," snarled Michael. "Antonia is a child."

"Many women are married at seventeen. You were born when your mother was not yet nineteen," Josef pointed out.

"But Antonia has led a sheltered life. She has no notion of the outside world."

Looking at his irate prince, Josef refrained from pressing the point. "I saw the princess earlier," he said instead. "We met in the corridor, but she did not speak to me. She immediately laid a finger to her lips and tiptoed past. Emily, the upstairs maid, was most puzzled."

Michael groaned. "Oh, no. I told Antonia to ignore me but otherwise to act normally. I should have known she would get caught up in her 'adventure.'"

THE COUNTESS AND THE BUTLER

Josef eyed Michael with curiosity. "Her adventure? What *are* you referring to?"

"Spying."

"Spying?"

"Yes, spying."

"On whom?"

"Heavens, I don't know. Ask Antonia." Then he looked at Josef with alarm. "No, don't do anything of the sort. I certainly don't want her to make more of the matter than she already has."

"*Why* is Princess Antonia spying?" asked Josef, trying a new tack.

Michael speared his fingers through his hair. "You may well ask," he said. "Actually, she believes that *I* am spying."

"You?"

"I."

Josef blinked. "Oh, I see. Ummm . . . whom are you spying on?"

"I have no idea. Except that my dear little sister feels—quite rightly, I will admit—that there should be *some* explanation for my impersonation of a butler. So, since she is unable to think of a reasonable one, she has decided I must be spying."

"Oh," said Josef, blinking. "How . . . original of the princess." He thought for a moment. "Indeed, there is certainly no reasonable explanation for your serving as a butler."

"Oh, no, don't you start on that again," Michael protested. "We've reviewed your objections far too many times. I was merely explaining why Antonia was tiptoeing past you with her finger to her lips. Antonia is a highly inventive child."

"Inventive, indeed," replied Josef. "Spies! Who else would have imagined spies at Amesworth Court?"

"Quite so," Michael affirmed.

Chapter Ten

Horace Poricy was most unhappy with the situation in which he found himself. He belatedly realized he had been mistaken to have succumbed the previous year to his urgent need for ready capital. Since he worked at the War Office, confidential documents circulated on a regular basis. It had seemed easy—then—to make a copy of Wellington's latest report and slip it into a dispatch bag. Later, he had "inadvertently" left the bag in a prearranged location.

It had been easier, anyway, than having to confess at White's that he was unable to pay his debts of honor. He would have been an outcast from fashionable Society if he had ever been forced to that ignoble point. No, it had been far simpler to do as the anonymous letter suggested and casually lose track of the dispatch bag while returning home. He had not known who received the dispatch, and he much preferred it that way. The money had appeared, as promised, and he had not thought beyond that.

Unfortunately, while Horace was very fond of gaming, he had deucedly bad luck at cards. So, here he was, twelve months later, in debt once again. This year, however, he had a chance of recouping his fortunes in a far more attractive way. It had been fortuitous that his friend Max Chesney had suggested that he visit Amesworth Court and meet the lovely young widowed countess.

True, Horace had never favored the idea of marriage. He had lived under the cat's paw of his mother for thirty-six years before she died, and that had been quite enough of the female sex for him. If he were to marry, however, then Natalie Chesney was certainly the perfect choice: beautiful, soft-spoken, wealthy. And while he was older than the countess, Alden Chesney had been much the same age, and she had married *him*. Horace had reason to believe he had the chance of a successful suit.

Then, just as everything seemed to be progressing well, the new letters had arrived. He had ignored the one that came to him in London, hoping that once he went off to Amesworth Court, nothing would come of it. But last night, his first night here, there had been another one. Another missive had been slipped under his pillow for him to find when he retired to bed. It informed him unnecessarily that he was deeply in debt, but it also declared that he was a traitor to his country, which he had, by dint of extreme mental effort, managed to forget. The tone of the letter was quite unnecessarily threatening, he thought. However, he could not ignore the final point: that he could be proven to be a traitor to his country. That dispatch copied in his handwriting *could* not be explained.

So Horace was slinking around the village inn and not at all pleased about the situation. "Meet me at the Fox and Hare in Abbingford Magna at nine tomorrow evening," the note had said. Horace peered into the taproom, where five or six bucolic-looking men in smocks were chugging down pints of ale. He blanched. What if the farmers or the innkeeper noticed him and mentioned his presence?

He faded back into the night—or at least hoped that he faded. It really was deucedly difficult for someone of his girth to slink or fade, he was finding. Backing up ponderously, he bumped into a rake. At least, he thought it was a rake. He was not very knowledgeable about farm implements.

"Damnation!" he snapped under his breath, rubbing his smarting calf and worrying about the damage his butter-soft Hessian boots might have sustained. He was very proud of his Hessians. He was very proud of all his wardrobe, actually, which was another reason his purse was always so much to let. And he was also much afraid that his valet might ask inconvenient questions if the boots became marred.

A window above him opened, and he shrank back out of the light, stepping into something soft and yielding that he thought it better not to question.

"Poricy!" hissed a low, commanding voice. "Stop making such a clamor down there and come up here. There's a stair to your left."

Horace realized that there was indeed an outside staircase leading to the second floor of the inn. Relieved, he hurried up it. Stepping inside, he blinked in the room's bright lantern light.

"Close the door behind you, you fool," the voice snapped.

Horace hurried to comply, then turned to look at the occupant of the room.

He was tall and of military bearing with short-cut steel gray hair and a hatchet-shaped face. Each sharply formed cheekbone bore a long scar, clearly the result of a sword or saber cut.

"Sit down," the man barked.

Again Horace hastily complied, though he summoned up enough nerve to ask, "Who are you?"

"If I decide there is reason for you to know that, then I will tell you," his companion snapped. "For now, you may address me as Count." His voice was curt with a slight accent Horace did not recognize. He didn't believe it was French, however, and that at least was a relief. He would hate to think he had sold state secrets to the French.

"Do you have the papers I requested?" the count demanded.

"No . . . No, I don't," Horace faltered. He was not a brave man, and this encounter was unnerving.

"Why not?"

"I didn't . . . I didn't think it was necessary."

"No?" The count's voice was steely, menacing. "I do not think that your government will look kindly upon a traitor, do you? You have been selling its secret documents to the enemy, Mr. Poricy. What would your superior Lord Castlereagh have to say if he were to know that?"

Horace blanched. "It would be your word against mine, Count," he said with false bravado. "I think Lord Castlereagh would believe *me*." But even as he made the avowal, he wondered what proof the count possessed. That worry had led him to the Fox and Hare tonight.

The stranger moved closer, towering over Horace. "Are you defying me?" he snarled. "You miserable little dog of an Englishman! Consorting with such a sniveling coward revolts me. If you don't do as I ask, I will spit you like a chicken. No, on second thoughts, I will not dishonor my sword so." Wrapping his long, strong fingers about Horace's neck, he exerted some pressure. "Oh, no, Mr. Poricy, you would never be safe again."

He squeezed a little harder, and Horace felt the breath choke in his throat and the blood pool in his head. He tried to protest, but he could not speak, could not even breathe.

"Bah!" The count pushed him away. "You see, Mr. Poricy? In mere moments you would have been no more. Are you still feeling defiant?"

"N-n-no," Horace choked.

"You will bring me the papers I requested tomorrow."

"Th-They are in London."

"You will make an excuse to return to London, then bring them back to me here."

"Y-yes."

"You may go now, you pitiful specimen," sneered the count. "If there were not a need for discretion, I would kick you down the stairs. Now go!"

Horace hastily complied.

"My dear countess," said Horace Poricy, "I regret to inform you that I have received an urgent summons to return to London." With an effort, he squeezed his considerable bulk under the breakfast table.

Looking at his plate, which he had loaded with eggs, rashers of bacon, several smoked kippers, and a large beefsteak, Natalie restrained an impolite shudder. Certainly if a gentleman was to spend the day walking his estate, whether inspecting the fields or hunting game, he needed a sizeable breakfast. But over the last two days Horace Poricy's idea of exercise had been a game of billiards, followed by several energetic rubbers of whist with Max. After that, both gentlemen, exhausted by their athletic endeavors, retired for a long afternoon nap in the library.

She realized what he had been saying. "London?" she echoed. "But you have just arrived, Mr. Poricy."

"Ah dear lady," he said with ponderous pride, "duty calls. Lord Castlereagh is in need of my assistance on a most important matter."

"Oh, well, then, of course," assured Natalie, wondering when Castlereagh's summons had come. She had heard nothing of a messenger arriving from London.

"But I engage to be back in mere days," said Mr.

Poricy. "I could not bear to miss more of your delightful house party . . . or your delightful self. And I would not want to think that I was spoiling your entertainments by my absence." He smiled in what he appeared to think was a flattering way.

Lord Anthony Darlington, who had been forking chunks of beefsteak into his mouth, spared a moment from his plate. "She doesn't need you here, Poricy," he said indistinctly around his last mouthful. "She's promised to ride with me today."

"I have?" said Natalie, startled. She didn't remember agreeing to anything of the sort. She supposed it was possible that she had not been paying attention as it was easy in present company to allow her thoughts to wander. Though the unmarried gentlemen had realized that a perpetual discourse on sporting events did not seem to be the way to win her attention, they now vacillated between discussing sports sporadically among themselves and ponderous attempts to woo her.

"I was planning to spend the morning on some accounts . . ." she began.

"Princess Antonia and I will be riding this morning," Vincent Delamere announced. "She tells me she is very fond of riding."

Michael Schmidt spoke up from his position near the sideboard. "Milady, Hughes sent up word from the stables that he would have horses for you and the princess saddled at eleven o'clock, as you requested. Do you wish me to send word back that he should ready horses for the gentlemen as well?"

Natalie stared blankly at Schmidt's handsome face. She had no memory of such a request. Yet her butler seemed certain that she had spoken with him on the matter.

Mr. Poricy was pouting visibly. "I am very sorry I will be disrupting your party for a few days," he said, his tone making clear his unhappiness that nobody seemed disturbed at all.

Natalie immediately soothed his ruffled feathers. "Oh, Mr. Poricy," she said, "I do hope you will return in time for the picnic I am planning on Thursday. We will be eating lunch at the temple on the promontory and viewing the lake."

"Yes, indeed," put in Lucretia, who had managed to make it down to breakfast today. Despite the balmy sunshine, she was wrapped in shawls lest a stray draft from the open windows chill her. "Dear Mr. Poricy, you must return for the picnic. The temple that my cousin, the late earl's father, had built is quite, quite lovely. I am told it exceeds in beauty even those of Greece and Rome. It is far newer, you see, with no fallen columns to mar its perfection."

Natalie was able to restrain herself from laughing, for she had heard Lucretia Dillerby's views on improving the historical wonders of the world. She thought she heard choking, however, across the table. She looked up and saw that Michael Schmidt, who was standing behind Lucretia, was in danger of losing a battle to hide his amusement.

Without thinking, she smiled at him, and she thought she saw an answering warmth in his pale gray eyes.

"Oh, yes, I see that my dear Natalie agrees with me," said Lucretia. "And the shrubbery there is quite spectacular also, Mr. Poricy. The late earl, as a young man, had the rhododendrons planted along the hillside, then pruned to allow intermittent glimpses of the spectacular beauty of the lake. Why, people travel for miles to see the lake at Amesworth. If I were not so prone to chills, I would walk there every day, I think, just to see such wild beauty."

"I will make every attempt to return by Thursday morning, or even Wednesday evening," said Mr. Poricy, puffing up with the attention now being paid him. He smiled at Natalie. "I would not want to miss such a promising outing, dear countess. I hope you will show me the views personally."

"And today you shall show them to me," stated Lord Anthony possessively.

"And me, too," said Mr. Hamilton and Lord Ashford simultaneously, clearly determined not to allow a rival an edge.

Natalie repressed a grimace. She really did need the time this morning to review her accounts, but she seemed to have been outmaneuvered. At least such a large group presented one distinct advantage: there was safety in numbers. As long as several of the gentlemen vied for her attention, she was unlikely to have to spend too much time with any one of them.

She did wonder, however, how she had ended up committed to this expedition. She glanced at Michael Schmidt. He was engaged with the serving dishes, but she thought she detected a small but smug smile. What could be going through his head? Really, he was a most puzzling butler.

Michael dragged Josef into the laundry room with him and closed the door.

Affecting a melodramatic sigh, he cast himself down in a chair and wiped his brow theatrically.

"Josef, I shall soon be quite distracted!" he exclaimed.

Josef regarded him unsympathetically. "What is your difficulty this time?" he asked dourly. "If you weren't masquerading as a common servant, perhaps you'd be having fewer troubles."

"Antonia is the trouble, of course," said Michael.

"And what mischief is Princess Antonia engaged in now? Is she still hunting spies?"

"No. That—thank heavens—seems to have gone out of her head. She's far too involved in flirting with a bounder who has designs on her virtue."

"Mr. Vincent Delamere, I presume," said Josef.

"Mr. Vincent Delamere," Michael confirmed with a growl. "I am at a loss to understand what can have gotten into my sister. She's always been sweet and biddable, so well-behaved." He jumped out of his chair and stalked across the room.

Josef regarded him with puzzlement. "Sweet? Biddable?" he queried. "Can we be speaking of the same princess? I'm thinking of the Princess Antonia who climbed out onto the parapets of Schloss Stell and had to be rescued by men with pitons and climbing ropes."

"Well, yes," agreed Michael. "But she's never been like *this*. So . . . so . . ." He stopped, flushing.

"So . . ." Josef prompted.

"So . . . flirtatious!" Michael said desperately.

Josef placed a compassionate hand on his shoulder. "My—Michael, the princess is seventeen years old. Like it or not, you need to understand that she's growing up. She's a young woman now."

"Still, she shouldn't have made an assignation to ride alone with that scoundrel Delamere," Michael said gruffly. "Who knows what he might attempt, given the opportunity?"

Josef looked slightly taken aback. "That is a problem. What are you going to do?"

"I've already done it," Michael said proudly. "The countess will be accompanying them."

"Ah, that's good," said Josef. Again, however, he looked puzzled. "How did you manage to arrange that?"

Michael grinned. "I'm afraid it's going to take some fast thinking to explain my actions to the countess, but so far I've managed to avoid doing so. I announced at breakfast that Hughes would have horses saddled for her and Toni at eleven, as she had requested."

Josef stared. "But the countess had not in fact requested these horses?"

"Oh, no," Michael said blithely. "I sent Oliver down to instruct Hughes directly after breakfast."

Josef gazed at him, fascinated. "Your highness never ceases to astonish me. Imagine, a butler secretly running this household by royal decree."

Michael shrugged. "Something needed to be done. I did it. But I do wonder how I'm going to explain it to the countess."

A knock sounded on the door, and both men jumped.

"Enter," called Michael.

The door opened, and Percy peered round it. "Oh, Mr. Schmidt," he said with relief, "here you are. I was about to ask Mr. Stern if he had any knowledge of your whereabouts. The countess is asking for you, sir."

Michael stood. "Where is she, Percy?"

"In the library, Mr. Schmidt."

Michael straightened his jacket. "Duty calls, then. Until later, Josef."

Walking along the narrow service corridor, he wondered what Natalie wished of him. An explanation, no doubt, he thought a tad uneasily.

When he opened the library door, she looked up from her large, leather-bound account book. "Ah, Schmidt, thank you for coming." She took off the little gold-framed glasses she wore for reading, then regarded him with a quizzical expression.

He waited.

"I am puzzled, Schmidt," she said finally.

He said nothing, though he had a good notion as to what puzzled her. He maintained an impassive demeanor.

"In fact, I am extremely puzzled," she continued after a moment.

Michael decided to help her—minimally. "You are, milady?"

"I do not remember expressing any intention of riding today. I had other plans entirely. I am certain I did not ask you to order horses for the princess and myself."

"You didn't request horses, milady?" Michael said, allowing a hint of puzzled inquiry to enter his own voice.

Natalie stared him down. "I did not ask you to order horses, Schmidt. I think you need to explain yourself."

Clearly, his blank-slate technique was not working. Now he was in a bind. In such circumstances, he had long believed, the solution was to stick as close to the truth as possible.

"Milady," he said slowly, thinking his way through the maze he had created. "I was concerned for the princess."

"For the princess," she echoed.

"She is a young girl, your ladyship, far from her homeland and her family. I grew up in her household; I remember the day she was born. Since she has no family here to care for her, I feel that I must assume some of that responsibility."

He could see understanding dawning on Natalie's lovely face. Encouraged, he repeated, "I was concerned, your ladyship. I did not feel it proper for the princess to ride alone with Mr. Delamere. I thought she should have some escort." He humbly cast down his gaze. "It was improper of me, milady, to speak for you, of course."

He stopped and waited. The Natalie he was coming to know was a compassionate woman, and he believed she would respond to his appeal.

When she spoke, her voice was indeed full of warmth. "Schmidt, you are entirely right. I should have realized it myself. I have been remiss in my duties as a hostess and a friend."

Michael looked up and saw that her blue eyes were

aglow. "How fortunate the von Stells were to have you in their service. And how fortunate my dear friend Antonia is to have you still at *her* service."

"It is nothing, milady," said Michael awkwardly.

She stood up and came around the desk. "No, no, Schmidt. You are too modest. I can only hope that one day *I* may inspire such loyalty."

"Countess, you already have it," he said impulsively, knowing suddenly that she did. But it was not the loyalty of which she spoke; it was something far warmer indeed. And no woman had ever made him feel quite this way before.

She was smiling at him still, her gaze locked with his. Did she, too, feel a connection between them?

He moved abruptly away from her and addressed her stiffly. "Will that be all, your ladyship? May I now return to my duties?"

She looked up at him with what appeared to be hurt in her blue-gray eyes. Still, he dared not let himself imagine any further sense of intimacy between them.

"Yes, that will be all, Schmidt. Thank you for the explanation," she said.

He bowed and left the room, uneasier than he had been upon entering it.

Chapter Eleven

*T*hursday dawned as bright and clear as Natalie had hoped it would. By eleven o'clock, the staff—who had been up since five preparing for the picnic—had three wagons loaded with the necessary supplies, which included tables, chairs, damask tablecloths, and china and silverware carefully packed into large wicker hampers. Not to mention, of course, the cold collation. This was not Natalie's notion of a simple meal *al fresco*, but it was what her guests expected.

At eleven-thirty, most of the company had assembled in the front hall. Those who would be walking stood in a cluster, and a barouche waited outside for those who preferred to be driven. The gentlemen had the additional option of riding; the ladies, however, all wished to wear their most delicate and enchanting muslin dresses as befit the festive occasion, so they would either walk or drive. Since Natalie was planning to walk, and Antonia had announced she would accompany her, most of the gentlemen exercised that option, as well.

At noon, the walking party finally left, having waited for Mr. Delamere, who apparently had been having trouble with his cravat. Although it was not a great distance—in fact Natalie quite often walked to the promontory and back before breakfast—Emily Seabury and Lucretia had elected to join elderly Aunt Abbie and Aunt Gracie in the barouche. Emily had divulged to Natalie that she was expecting "a little package," as she expressed it, early next year, and as a result was feeling a trifle under the weather.

Cousin Jane and her husband had elected to walk. This news caused Natalie to consider escaping to the barouche, but she decided, especially given her conversation with Schmidt, that she really should chaperone Antonia. While Toni's behavior certainly never crossed the line into scandalous, she was flirting a trifle more than was proper for a girl of seventeen. Since she was also having a great deal of innocent fun, perhaps for the first time in her rather restricted life, Natalie was reluctant to call a halt to it, particularly since Toni had confided that she was due to make a dynastic marriage soon. Natalie did want to make sure, however, that her young friend remained safe and her comportment never became open to comment. Both as her hostess and as a more mature friend, she felt responsibility to the girl, who was, as it had taken her butler to remind her, in a foreign land without family supervision.

As they walked, the group soon separated. Most of the gentlemen strode along together, talking with animation of fox hunting, fishing and other generally masculine pursuits. Max and Matilda walked arm in arm at a sedate pace that the others soon outstripped, which undoubtedly was fine with the cozy pair. For a while, Raymond Hargrave and Jane accompanied Antonia and Delamere, boring them with a discussion of the wonders of English mycology, and, to her relief, leaving Natalie to walk on her own.

Shortly, however, Raymond stopped to examine an unusual toadstool he noticed beside the path, and Antonia and Delamere seized the opportunity to walk ahead. Jane, however, dropped back to join Natalie.

"The way that girl behaves is quite scandalous, Natalie," Jane remarked. Antonia had furled her parasol and was gently poking Delamere in feigned indignation at some sally of his.

Natalie gazed at her cousin. "I certainly would not say it was scandalous, Jane," she replied mildly.

"I would," said Jane. "I never liked her at school. Such vulgar exuberance. Honestly, if she weren't a princess, I would call her ill-bred. I think you really must speak to her, Natalie. I find it most uncomfortable to be forced to associate with her."

An angry retort simmered in Natalie's throat, but she had learned that arguing with Jane was useless and usually caused unfortunate repercussions—for Natalie. She pressed her lips together firmly and walked on in silence. Out of the corner of her eye, she could see that her cousin was about to speak again. Fortunately, though, at that moment, Jane's husband summoned her, and she hurried to his side.

A few moments later, Lord Anthony Darlington noticed for the first time that their hostess was walking on her own, and he left the group of gentlemen to join her. Within minutes, Mr. Hamilton and Lord Ashford also hastened to her side, manfully vying to boast to her of who among them had made the greatest run or most spectacular jump astride the best piece of horseflesh. Natalie resigned herself to boredom. Max's scheme for this house party was certainly doing nothing to alter her intention to live on her own at the dower house. Perhaps it was some fault in herself that she found so few of the gentlemen of her acquaintance interesting. Giles and Alden had been the two exceptions. She wondered why the image of her butler suddenly sprang to her mind as another exception.

*   *   *

Michael paused in overseeing the reloading of the picnic supplies into the wagons and allowed himself to take a brief, self-congratulatory respite. He thought the *al fresco* meal had gone off very well indeed. By the time the guests had arrived at the reproduction Grecian temple, the long trestle tables had been set up on the fine-mown green sward, covered with pristine white cloths and laid with the china and silver. The collation, while cold, had been replete with sliced meats and numerous jellies and trifles, all of which had survived transport from the house. In all, a successful affair.

True, he had been annoyed to see Antonia, arriving at the head of the walking party, arm in arm with that scoundrel Delamere. He was going to have to find an opportunity to speak seriously with her on the matter. Their mother would have been shocked to see that her strict lessons on propriety had not taken with her younger child.

Antonia! He realized with a nasty jolt that he hadn't seen her in some minutes. He glanced around. The ladies and gentlemen had separated into small groups and were strolling about, some investigating the temple, others standing at the edge of the hill looking down toward the lake. Antonia was nowhere to be seen. Neither was Vincent Delamere.

Attempting to appear nonchalant, Michael walked around the temple, checking both inside and around the back, but he was unable to locate his sister.

He approached Oliver. "The party seems to have split up," he said to the footman in a purposefully neutral tone. "Have you any idea where the rest of the guests may have strayed?"

"I believe a couple of them went down the hill to look at the old earl's American garden," said Oliver. "It's famous in these parts. I heard tell as a child how he had mountains of earth brought in from other parts so those foreign trees would grow. Quite a sight, my mam used to say—streams of horses pulling drays filled with earth. Went on for years, she said. I dunno. Just looks like trees to me."

Michael was fretting, wishing Oliver had not chosen this moment to become loquacious. He dared not cut him off, for fear of seeming unduly involved with the countess's guests.

"Is that so?" he said when Oliver paused to draw a breath. "Well, the American garden certainly does sound interesting. I shall have to view it sometime."

He then resumed overseeing the final loading of the wagons, which did not take long, and sent them off under Oliver's supervision.

Left to himself at last, he set off down the slope in the direction of the American garden. Antonia and Delamere had not returned, and it was at least fifteen minutes since he had last seen her. He was out of his mind with worry, and what he wanted to do to Delamere didn't bear mentioning!

Natalie looked about her. When had she last seen Antonia? It must have been quite some minutes previously. She supposed it was inevitable that Vincent Delamere was not in sight either. After her discussion with Michael and Jane's pointed remarks, Natalie was feeling especially sensitive about preventing Antonia's behavior from causing comment. While Antonia's flirting was not truly out of line, it would be more discreet of the girl not to allow one man to be so particular in his attentions.

After a moment's thought, she remembered that the two had been discussing the American garden, which lay directly down the hill between the temple and the lake. Antonia had sounded intrigued by it and must surely have gone with Delamere to see it.

Natalie wished she could merely slip off on her own to investigate, but since she was the hostess, that would never do. The fresh air seemed to have set off Lucretia's breathlessness, so she had returned to the house. Max and Matilda had wandered away sometime earlier. A few comments carefully placed amidst the rest of the party, however, roused interest in the American garden, and soon Natalie was walking down the hill with her usual court of unmarried men. She was wearying of their ceaseless escort, she thought crossly, and wished there were some way of sending them away. The scheme that Max had thought so clever was turning out just as badly as she had ever feared.

What was called the American garden was actually a carefully tended wood, with winding paths curling around large evergreen trees, and azalea and rhododendron bushes. At intervals, one encountered marble statuary and benches set into recesses in the shrubbery. In the spring, when the azaleas and rhododendrons bloomed, the wood was delightfully colorful, and nearby was a lovely meadow filled with what she had been told was Virginia bluebell. This late in the summer, however, the garden was dark and dim, and Natalie was not sure it was worth the considerable effort required to keep the plants flourishing so far from their native habitat.

The group meandered down a path that led toward the lake. Natalie kept her eyes open and listened intently but saw and heard nothing of Antonia or Delamere. Upon reaching the lake, however, John Hamilton and Lord Ashford noticed a fish jumping some distance from shore. They instantly became immersed in discussing fishing and the possibility of reappearing with rods and reels early the next morning in order to try their luck.

Natalie was too concerned about Antonia to stand patiently for masculine chatter that showed no signs of end-

ing any time in the next hour. She accepted the escort of
her remaining suitor, Lord Anthony, and continued along
the verge of the lake until the path once again wound
back into the woods.

As they entered a pleasant glade with a stream mean-
dering through it, however, she realized that Lord Anthony was leaning considerably closer to her than she
liked. She moved slightly, putting some distance between
them, but he immediately closed it. A minute later, he slid
his hand from where it was supporting her elbow and
placed it on her waist.

Natalie stopped, realizing suddenly that she was alone,
away from the others, with a London man-about-town
she did not know very well. In her concern over Antonia's circumstances, she had placed herself in a similar
situation.

"Lord Anthony," she said in the most chilling tone she
could manage, "I think perhaps we should return now."

He smiled. "Oh, Hamilton and Ashford will be talking
fishing for hours yet. Surely you and I have better ways
to amuse ourselves."

There was a bench beside them. He sat, pulling Natalie
down next to him. "See," he said, "it is sunny here, and
the birds are singing. We can admire nature together, and
I can admire something even lovelier." He placed one
hand on her knee. "You are a charming woman, my dear,
and you are winning my heart. How can I show you the
admiration and esteem in which I hold you?"

"You can take me back to the picnic," Natalie said
crossly.

"Oh, surely you don't want to do that. It was clever of
you to lose Hamilton and Ashford so handily. You seem
so demure, my dear, that it took me some time to realize
your plan."

Natalie stared at him. Did he really believe she had

brought him here for a tryst? While she did not think her behavior in the least suggestive, a supremely self-satisfied man might see it that way. She was growing concerned. She certainly did not want to cause a scene with one of her guests, but Lord Anthony was not taking a hint easily. How could both of them emerge with their dignity intact?

Michael was hot and cross. He had been combing the woods for some fifteen minutes and still saw no sign of his errant sister and her persistent suitor. He was hesitating at yet another intersection in the winding paths when he heard a peal of laughter. It was clearly Antonia's, and it sent a chill down his spine, for he detected a faint undertone of fear in it.

Charging down the path that led in the direction of the laughter, he was spurred on by his sister's voice saying, "Oh, no, Vincent, you really, really mustn't."

There was an ominous pause, and then Antonia's voice rang out again. "Vincent, no! I have said you must not. I do *not* think this is proper."

Michael dashed round a corner and beheld Delamere, flushed and panting slightly. Antonia's hat was askew, the fichu of her dress not quite straight. She was holding Delamere at a distance with the point of her parasol.

Michael swore silently at the sight, but he applauded his little sister as well. In her own inimitable way, Antonia was in control of the situation.

Michael slowed to a walk, smoothing his own clothes imperceptibly. "Princess Antonia," he called.

She started. "Mi . . . I mean Schmidt, whatever are you doing here?"

"Princess," he said firmly. "I cannot believe that the prince, your brother, would approve of your being alone with a gentleman."

She gazed at him. "No," she said slowly, "no. I suppose he would not." She smiled widely. "Perhaps you could escort me back to the others, Schmidt."

She turned to Vincent Delamere. "I believe you are free to leave us now, Mr. Delamere," she said in the royal tone of voice she seldom assumed. "Schmidt, here, who has been in the service of my family for many years, will escort me back to the picnic." With regal grace, she sailed over to Michael and rested her hand on the arm he extended to her.

Delamere stared at them for several moments. Then, with a muffled curse, he strode down a different path.

Antonia dimpled up at Michael and switched to speaking German. "I don't think Mr. Delamere is very pleased with me, dearest."

"I am extremely *glad* that Mr. Delamere is not pleased with you, Toni," Michael said. "You have been behaving shamelessly, and have only now apparently regained your sanity. I am not very pleased with you myself."

She hung her head. "I'm sorry, Michael. It's not been much fun being me the last few months. I don't like the thought of marrying that awful Bonaparte cousin, and I don't understand what's happening between you and Carl Friedrich or why you are spying." She clung to his arm. "Michael, really, I am terribly worried. Are you in any danger?"

He wrapped an arm about her and kissed her forehead. "Toni, dearest, you mustn't worry. I'm fine and I'll take care of you, I promise."

She smiled up at him, her usual merry gleam returning to her eyes. "Of course you will, Michael. You always take care of everything. I don't know why I worried, even for a moment."

He hugged her tightly, holding her close for a moment. "That's my girl. Now, come along, naughty one. Let's return you to the others. And I want you to promise me that you will never flirt so outrageously again."

She giggled. "It was fun, Michael. Right up to the end, anyway, when he was trying to kiss me. When I squirmed away, his lips ended up sliding all over my face. That was rather slimy, I thought."

Michael growled, and she immediately made a penitent face. "I'm sorry, Michael dear, I won't do it again, I promise. I see now why we were always warned at school against encouraging young men. Mr. Delamere got quite the most ridiculous notions. I'm glad I had my parasol along."

Michael laughed. "A parasol, indeed. You are inimitable, Toni."

"Well," said Antonia firmly, "he shouldn't have tried to kiss me when I didn't want to be kissed."

"That is quite true," said Michael, tucking Antonia's hand into his and patting it as if she were four years old again. "Come along now, Toni."

"Lord Anthony," said Natalie severely. "You must escort me back to the others."

"But I want to marry you," Lord Anthony protested. "You are everything I have ever looked for in a wife— young, lovely, well-born . . ."

And well-to-do, Natalie added silently, for she thought that might be the primary cause of the young man's precipitous passion.

"But I see I must convince you of what I am saying," said Lord Anthony. "Natalie, I am hopelessly, desperately in love with you."

He unexpectedly wrapped his arms around her and kissed her. Natalie struggled against the unwanted embrace, but he used his superior strength to immobilize her, pressing her shoulders painfully against the hard, cold stone of the bench. She freed her lips enough to cry out in protest, but Lord Anthony took no notice.

Abruptly, she felt herself released. Seconds later, she heard a loud splash. She looked up, still slightly dazed, to see her butler, Michael Schmidt, standing furious guard over the shallow stream in which Lord Anthony now sat. Clearly, Michael had plucked him from the bench and thrown him there. The warrior wrath on Michael's face was frightening, and Natalie could almost imagine a fiery sword in his hand. Apparently, Lord Anthony felt the same way, for he made no attempt to stand and challenge the butler until Michael, with a disgusted movement of his hand, motioned him to rise.

His clothes dripping, Lord Anthony stood. "I say, my man," he bleated, "what concern is it of yours . . . The lady and I . . ."

"The lady was requesting you to stop," Michael said coldly.

At that moment, however, Lord Anthony suddenly registered who Michael was, and his jaw dropped.

"You!" he said. "You . . . you're the . . . the butler. How dare you lay hands on me? I will have you dismissed immediately."

"You will do nothing of the sort," said Natalie, in a cold fury. Earlier, she had been anxious to avoid a scene, but the situation was past that point.

She stood up from the bench and confronted Lord Anthony. "How dare *you* lay hands on me in such a fashion? I have never been so insulted in my life. You cannot possibly have thought that I would encourage such behavior when I was clearly telling you that I was not interested. You will do me the courtesy of leaving me now, and I trust that upon returning to the house you will find that another engagement is urgently calling you away from Amesworth Court. I expect to hear that you are gone by dinnertime."

Lord Anthony blanched before the outpouring of her wrath. As soon as she was finished, he made as hasty an exit as his sodden clothing allowed.

Natalie sank down to the bench, feeling a trifle wobbly about the knees, and buried her face in her hands. Now that it was over, she was feeling a little sick.

She heard a rush of slippered feet across the grass, and then felt a feminine hand gently patting her back.

"Oh, Nini, darling, are you all right? I was so worried. But wasn't Michael wonderful? Didn't you think he was just splendid?" asked Antonia.

Natalie looked up. Antonia sat nestled beside her on the bench, with Michael Schmidt standing by, looking stiff and rather uncomfortable.

"I forgot," Natalie said, "that the two of you must know each other. But, of course you do, Toni, for you called Schmidt by his Christian name just now."

Antonia opened her mouth as if to reply, but Michael Schmidt cut in.

"Her highness is kind enough to bear a fondness for me from her childhood. I am fortunate to be allowed the chance to serve her once again."

"But what are the two of you doing down here?" asked Natalie. "Half the occupants of my house seem to be wandering about in this shrubbery."

"I came upon her highness in a situation where she needed escort," said Michael, "so I offered to accompany her back to the rest of the party."

Natalie smiled warmly. "That was certainly very kind of you." She paused. "And I appreciate your help here, as well," she added a little awkwardly.

"It was nothing, milady. I am glad to be of assistance," said Michael.

Once again, he was the perfect butler—stoic, humble,

impassive. She wondered if she had imagined the warrior king she had seen a few moments previously.

"I thank you all the same," she said, perplexed that she should feel on edge with a man who was merely her servant. "Well, I must be returning to our party. And Mr. Schmidt, surely you have duties to attend to as well. Antonia, will you accompany me? Neither of us should have been down here alone without the other guests," she admitted.

Silently, Michael fell in behind the two ladies as a proper servant should.

Chapter Twelve

All his life Michael had been an early riser. At home in Estavia, the hours before others awoke was his time to escape temporarily the rigors and restrictions of royalty. Now, having committed himself to what he was coming to believe was the most difficult undertaking of his life, playing a menial to a lovely lady, he found once again that the silence before dawn permitted him to relax.

At this time in the morning, it was dark and quiet in the basement kitchen. Upstairs in the attics, the maids and footmen would be sleepily starting to dress. For now, however, Michael had the place to himself. After using a poker to stir up the glowing embers of last night's fire in Amesworth Court's modern closed stove, he replenished it with fresh wood. Then he quietly went about a few duties until the stove grew hot enough to boil a kettle. Finally he settled comfortably at the kitchen table with a steaming cup of tea close at hand.

In these solitary moments, he didn't have to worry about appearance or comportment. Later, before the kitchen maids appeared, he would return upstairs and finish dressing. For now, he could slouch in his shirtsleeves, his shoes kicked off. The day promised to be warm, so it was pleasant to be free of his coat.

He propped his stockinged feet up on another chair

and leaned back. He had brought along a book to read—
Marlborough's account of his military campaigns during
the previous century, which Michael had found in
Amesworth Court's library—but he left it lying in his
lap.

Yesterday had produced many surprises. Some were
good, for he thought that Toni had learned her lesson
about injudicious flirting. She was clearly shocked by the
results of the encouragement she had given Vincent Delamere, and Michael believed she would be more circumspect in the future.

What had shocked *him*, however, was how *he* had reacted to the various events of the day.

Yes, he had been angry at Delamere, but not unrea-
sonably so. He had been able to give level-headed consideration to the matter and form a plan that would allow
him to rescue Antonia and still keep his true identity hidden. He had remained the calm man of reason he prided
himself on being.

But the rage he had felt when he saw Natalie struggling in Lord Anthony's embrace was something else entirely, stunning him with its intensity. He had not stopped
to think whether or not a butler would interrupt such a
scene. Instead, he had acted on impulse. It was immediately obvious to him that Natalie was unhappy and frightened, and he had reacted with a burning desire to save her
from any further distress. Only when he was standing
over the dripping Lord Anthony had he realized that his
behavior was out of character for a butler.

A true servant, seeing the lady of the house locked in
an embrace with one of her guests, would have discreetly
turned the other way. Instead, he had dared to lay hands
on a member of the nobility. He was fortunate his employer hadn't considered his impulsive actions cause for
instant dismissal.

Thinking of her, he smiled involuntarily. She was an enchanting study in contrasts—a poised, charming chatelaine confident in her ability to manage her household, yet with a poignant innocence about her. From the gossip of the staff, he knew that she had grieved deeply after the death of her husband. Still, he sensed something more than grief. She fascinated him, this vulnerable countess. He wished circumstances had been such that he could know her as an equal.

Natalie awoke earlier than usual, but, stretching in her bed, she felt strange, indefinable restlessness. She wanted to do something active and new and unusual. She felt as though her life was changing, though she didn't know how or why.

The first light of day was creeping around the thick brocade curtains covering the tall windows in her bedchamber. Climbing from the bed, she crossed the room and slid between the heavy curtains and the window itself. The sky was beginning to gleam with streaks of pearly pink and orange, and she couldn't see a trace of clouds. She opened the window and cool air flowed in, caressing her neck where the ruffle of her nightgown ended, and whispering along her bare toes and ankles. The birds were in full dawn chorus. It was going to be a beautiful morning, and suddenly she knew she couldn't wait another moment to be a part of it.

She could have called her maid, but that would have been unkind. A glance at the gilt and china clock on the mantelpiece told her that it was not yet five. Rummaging through the wide shelves of her wardrobe where Gwyneth kept the dresses carefully laid out in pristine condition, she found a simple gown that she could don without aid. It would be suitable for her impulsive plan to pick raspberries in the home farm meadows. They would

eat raspberries with cream for luncheon in polite splendor
in Natalie's drawing room, and none of the guests would
ever know that it was their hostess who had picked them.

Hastily, she donned the dress, then tied a white fichu
around her neck, and pulled a simple cotton cap over her
hair. She didn't want to wake anyone, so she carried her
shoes and stockings as she crept out of her room. She tiptoed down the servants' stairs to the kitchen, where a
small door—far quieter and easier to open than the big
formal front door—led out to the kitchen garden. Nobody would be in the kitchen yet, though up in the attics
the kitchen maids might be stirring.

She opened the door to the kitchen and stopped, for the
fire was burning merrily and a lamp glowed on the table.
Leaning back in one straight chair, with his legs balanced
on another, was her butler, as shoeless as she was, reading a book that sat on his lap and sipping tea from a pot-
tery cup.

His white cotton shirt was only partly buttoned and
loosely tucked into his knee breeches. Had she ever seen
a man's bare chest before? Well, Alden's, but mostly
glimpsed through his nightshirt as she tended him after
his seizure. And she had seen shirtless laborers in the
fields at harvest time, but that was from a distance, and
not men she knew well.

For a moment, she was mesmerized by the sight of
Michael's chest—the vee of skin revealed by the open
shirt. Then her cheeks flamed with embarrassment at the
direction of her thoughts, and in her confusion she
dropped a shoe.

Michael looked up.

"Your ladyship," he said, startled. "What are you doing
here?" He stood and quickly began buttoning his shirt.

She stared again, fascinated by those tapered fingers
fitting each pearly button into its correct hole.

In a moment, he was more properly covered, although his coat remained draped on another chair. His gaze dropped to her ankles, and she suddenly remembered her own shoeless, stockingless state.

"Excuse me," she muttered and darted out the door into the hallway, where she hurriedly pulled on her stockings and shoes. What could her butler have thought of such a breach of propriety?

Refusing to be intimidated, she returned to the kitchen. She would need a basket for the raspberries, and the door she wished to use was in that room as well.

Michael was rinsing his cup at the big stone sink.

"Milady," he said, "may I help you?"

"I'm going to pick raspberries," she declared. "I will need a basket."

He frowned. "Do you wish me to summon a maid or a footman to attend you? I can . . ."

"No, no," she said hastily. "They have their own duties and I'm going on my own."

"Alone, milady? No, no, your ladyship. I will fetch one of the footmen. It will take but a few minutes."

"I don't want anyone," she insisted. "I am quite capable of going outdoors on my own."

She stopped speaking. Was he ignoring her? He had turned his back and was slipping on his coat and shoes.

"Then I will escort you," he said.

Without further argument—for she knew as well as he that it was not completely safe for a woman alone, especially at such an early hour—she reached for a basket and led the way outdoors.

As they emerged into the walled kitchen garden which lay between the house and the stable block, she took a deep breath of the fresh, sparkling morning air, feeling it surge through her veins like the tingle of champagne. The gloriously warm summer weather had caused the beans to run rampant on their poles, their scarlet blooms splendidly vivid against the dark green of the leafy vines. At her feet, the neat rows of lettuces and the bountiful fronds of the carrots were testimony to the fertility of the soil and the excellent care of the gardeners. Natalie looked about her appreciatively.

"In its own way, the sight is as beautiful as that of a rose garden, is it not?" said Michael quietly from beside her.

She smiled up at him. "Yes," she agreed. "I love the brilliance of the bean flowers especially."

"Is that what they are?" he asked. "I didn't know."

She laughed. "Did your family not grow a vegetable garden?"

She saw him hesitate, as if choosing his words, and wondered why he felt it necessary to be so careful. Then she remembered that he was her servant. She had been so at ease for a moment, she had forgotten that he was not her social equal.

"We can go out this way," she said, leading him through the onion beds to a small arched door in the brick wall on the far side. She twisted the ring in the wooden door and let them out onto the graveled drive just beyond the stable yard.

The route she chose led across a short stretch of the park, and then down over the four-foot drop that kept the cows that grazed in the fields of the home farm from straying into the park. Michael jumped down easily, demonstrating the athletic ease and grace that she had noted before. Idly, she thought he seemed very suited to the outdoors. Strange in a man whose duties kept him inside much of the time.

Natalie was perfectly capable of getting down, too, but she knew from previous experience that the feat involved first sitting on the edge of the timber-banked wall—not the most graceful of acts with an interested observer standing below. She hesitated on the edge.

There was laughter in Michael's gray eyes.

"Jump," he said, holding out his arms. "I'll catch you."

She thought of ignoring him but found herself unable to resist the challenge. What was happening to her quiet, staid self? she wondered. Setting her basket down and flinging caution to the winds, she leapt from the edge and felt his muscular arms catch and hold her.

In a flash, she remembered the day she had met him, when she had nearly fallen from the library desk. The strength of his arms, the sense of restrained power, the intense masculinity—all were still there. But this time she was alone with him, no footman to chaperone her.

Her breath caught in her throat, and her heart started to race.

His arms tightened around her. He lowered his head, and for a moment she imagined that he was about to kiss her. She remembered the day she had first met him, when she had reprimanded him for daring to kiss her hand. She knew that she should reprove him now. He was a servant, and she was his employer.

Yet a part of her was loath to do so. She was a woman, after all, and it had been a long time since a man had kissed her. She had felt passion when Giles and she had stolen kisses in the few moments they had been able to be alone together. She had expected to feel fulfillment in the marriage bed with Alden—was sure she would have done so if illness had not felled him. And yet for three years she had walled herself off from all such emotion. She had been a caring, loving nurse for Alden as he slowly wasted away. She had been the proper, respectable, grief-stricken widow for the year of mourning that followed his death.

She longed to be more than that, to bring back to life

the eager young girl she had suppressed. What would it be like to feel a man's lips on hers again? She longed to break free of the restrictive conventions surrounding her.

Michael released her, placing her carefully on the ground.

"See," he said lightly, "it was not so big a jump."

She smiled and nodded weakly in response. Had she imagined that moment when she thought he would kiss her? Perhaps. And yet feminine instinct told her that she had not. If she were truly the sensible woman she believed herself to be, she would not continue on alone with him. She would return to the house and seek a maid or footman to accompany her. She didn't feel like being prudent and sensible, however. She picked up her basket and started down the path.

When she reached them, the raspberry bushes were laden with fruit, the plump berries bending the thorny branches nearly to the ground. Placing her basket next to her, Natalie started to pick, carefully ignoring Michael's silent but palpable presence behind her. The raspberries were exquisite, ruby-colored jewels still glistening with the dew and releasing a perfume redolent of summer. She inhaled deeply and appreciatively as she filled her basket.

After some time, she noticed that the basket was filling faster than she expected. At that moment, her fingers brushed someone else's. Looking down in surprise, she saw a masculine hand depositing a pile of berries into the basket.

Her gaze flew up. Michael smiled at her briefly, then turned back to the bushes and commenced picking again. Natalie watched in surprise. She hadn't asked for assistance. Why was he not standing back properly, as a well-trained footman would? But then Michael Schmidt often threw her off balance by behaving in an unexpected manner.

She shrugged and started picking again. Many, many berries dotted the bushes, and she had brought a large basket. She decided she would ask Cook to make raspberry fool for dinner tonight. Even with the large house party to feed, if she and Michael filled the basket between them, the kitchen staff could make jam as well.

They continued in silence, the warm sun on their shoulders. Natalie could hear the buzzing of the bees as they, too, started their day's work. From a distance came the lowing of the home farm cows as they went in for their morning milking. Occasionally, as she and Michael picked, their hands would brush again, or their shoulders touch for a moment. She found the casual intimacy strangely pleasant.

Finally, the basket was full—a great heap of pristine, perfect berries. With a sigh of satisfaction, Natalie dropped to the grass and rubbed a hand across her face.

"Oh, I'm hot and tired," she said. "I think it's going to be warm today." She looked up at Michael. "You sit, too," she offered spontaneously. "You must need a respite, as well. Picking raspberries is hot work."

He smiled and sat down on the grass beside her. "How very English this is here," he said.

"Do you not have raspberries in Estavia?" she asked.

"Oh, yes, we do, but it would be in a very different setting." He looked at the green, rolling fields around them. "Estavia is on the edge of the Alps, you know. We have steep hills covered with dark forests, leading up to snow-covered mountaintops. If we went to pick raspberries, it would be to the forest, in a sunny glade, perhaps backing up against a large rock outcropping."

Natalie was fascinated. "You make it sound very beautiful," she said. "I can almost see it. I wish I could see it in truth."

She looked down at her hands. "I have never been outside England. My mother was French, and she used to tell me tales of her childhood in Anjou and promise that, when her family's lands were restored to them, we would go there to see the chateau where she grew up. But it never happened. She and my father both died when I was twelve years old. And her family's lands have not been restored. I am not actually sure that there is anyone for them to be restored to. My grandfather and grandmother perished in the Terror, as did my mother's brother. My mother was the only one to escape, and she was lucky to do so. I suppose that if the monarchy were ever restored, then I might inherit the lands. I don't know."

She stopped with an embarrassed laugh, then looked at Michael. He was sitting with his hands wrapped around his knees, listening to her gravely. "I'm babbling," she said. "You cannot possibly be interested."

"Oh, but I am," he replied.

"I would like to see France someday," she said, "though that seems unlikely to happen anytime soon, with Bonaparte loose in Europe. But at the very least, it would be nice to see more of England. I have never even been north of Shrewsbury," she admitted with a laugh, "and that is not very far north at all. I long to see more."

He smiled in sympathy, but said, "Are you not finding the grass wet to sit upon?"

Natalie shifted and realized that the morning dew was indeed soaking through her skirt.

Michael took off his coat and spread it out on the grass. "Sit here," he said.

She might have protested, but his oddly masterful tone had her complying. She moved onto the coat.

"But what about you?" she asked when he stayed where he was. "You must be feeling the damp, too."

"I'll be fine," he said.

"No, come sit here. There's room for two."

There *was* room for two, though it was a narrow space. His shirtsleeved arm brushed against hers, but she did not move away from the intimacy.

"How I envy you the chance to travel to different countries," she said. "Is Estavia still your favorite?"

His eyes softened. "I think it is the most beautiful country in the world. It is small, you know, much smaller even than this country. But it has fast-running crystal streams, and great, dark forests in which the wild boars still roam, and rocky mountain crags capped by snow. And Stellberg . . ." He paused, and sighed. "Well, I have never seen anywhere quite as lovely as Stellberg. The entire city is clustered around a great rock, on which the old castle was built, from the days in which my—from the days in which our royal family's ancestors were robber barons, preying on the travelers who came on the road from Vienna. Those were the bad, old days. But for all that we are a country with a grand and illustrious past. To see it all threatened now—"

He broke off, and she looked up at him. His eyes were hard, and steely. "Why, what is wrong?" she asked.

"If that usurper Bonaparte has his way, our heritage will vanish as if it never was," he said. "It will be like, poof!"—he snapped his fingers—"a candle in the wind. One breath from the emperor of France, and we will be extinguished."

Natalie had seldom heard anyone speak with such passion of his country. But, then, of course, she thought, England had never been threatened that way. Yes, there had been talk of invasion in the early years of the century, when she was still in the schoolroom, but she did not think that even then anyone had truly believed it would happen. She looked up in compassion at Michael's stern face, set now into hard lines.

"You care very deeply," she said softly.

"Yes."

She hated the look of sadness she saw. She leaned toward him. "I am sorry," she said quietly. "It must be very painful for you."

He looked down at her, and suddenly she was intensely aware of his chiseled lips close to hers.

He lowered his head, and she raised hers. His lips were cool and firm and questing. She nestled against him, and his arms went around her. Held hard against the heart beating so powerfully in the strong wall of his chest, she felt a sense of rightness.

His lips left hers almost reluctantly. She looked up at him through half-closed, dazed eyes.

Abruptly, he stood, his manner formal again. "Milady, I apologize," he said. "I cannot imagine what came over me."

She looked up at him and felt she had momentarily lost her grip on what was real and what was not.

This was her butler whom she had been kissing. With a gasp, she jumped to her feet as well. She flushed hotly. What could she have been thinking?

"I think we should return to the house now, milady," said Michael Schmidt, stooping to pick up the basket of raspberries.

Mutely she acquiesced, following him in silence as he strode down the path that led back to the manor house.

Chapter Thirteen

*I*n the hours that followed, Natalie accomplished her daily duties in a daze. In her imagination she could still feel the pressure of Michael's mouth on her lips.

It was ironic, she thought, that she should feel this way. Here she was, no longer young, a mature woman. A widow, for heaven's sake. And yet she knew very little of what happened between a man and a woman.

Of course, she and Giles had kissed all those long years ago. They had been young and in love and she had felt then the same wild hotness running through her blood when they secretly embraced. But they had never gone further than kisses.

Alden had kissed her, too, gently and very comfortingly, after they had decided they would marry. She had felt no heat when he embraced her, but he had assured her that would come later, in the marriage bed, and she had believed him. "I am no young hotblood to make love to you on an uncomfortable bench in a garden," he had said, laughing and stroking her hair. "I prefer to make love to my wife in comfort, in a soft bed with a feather mattress and pillows to support her."

But there had been no later. During the week before their wedding, her courses had been delayed—nervousness had that effect on her—and came finally on her wedding night, so they waited. Two days later, Alden was felled by apoplexy.

So, here she was, a widowed virgin. It was an irony of which no one else was aware. She remembered, shortly after they had wed, Lucretia asking whether there was any chance she might be bearing an heir for Alden. At the time, Natalie had only felt grief over the child who would never be. Now, however, she found herself reflecting on the act of lying with a man. She knew so little about it.

She entertained a fantasy of disdaining the bounds of propriety and engaging in a discreet affair with Michael Schmidt. She had no wish to marry again. She hated London. She hated fashionable Society. She was happy, the quiet mistress of her small domain. Marriage meant surrendering to a man who could make her happy or unhappy by his whim. When she married Alden, she had been escaping the oppressive bondage of her aunt and uncle. But now she was her own woman, free at last, and had no interest in taking such a risk again.

The thought of tasting the delights of the flesh, however, suddenly seemed very enticing. She felt blood heating her cheeks at the very notion. Since the world assumed her a maiden no longer, it could not hurt her if she lost her virginity at last. With Michael, a man whose class was so far beneath hers that he could have no thoughts of marriage with her, she would be safe. Her butler could scarcely use a liaison with her to trap her into matrimony.

Without thinking why she was doing so, she had already instructed Gwyneth to lay out the most alluring of her evening gowns, a soft pale blue silk that was cut low across her bosom and clung to her waist and thighs.

"I'll wear the pearls tonight, Gwyneth," she said now, looking at herself in her mirror.

Taking the triple strand from her maid, she fastened them around her neck and felt the large, cool globes settle against the top swell of her breasts, almost like the touch of a man's fingers. She looked at them in the mirror, the bottommost pearl just nestling at the beginning of her cleavage, and admitted to herself that she looked lovely tonight. Her eyes were shining, and her cheeks were bright with color.

She looked like a woman going to meet her lover.

She thought of Michael, of how handsome he looked in his black coat and knee breeches, of how his broad shoulders filled out the coat, and how his calves swelled with muscle below the knee band of the breeches.

She wondered if *he* would think her beautiful tonight. She wondered if she had the courage to take a lover.

Picking up a pale blue and gilt fan, she stood and prepared to go downstairs.

She was lovely. She was quite the most alluring woman he had ever seen. Standing in proper fashion at the sideboard, overseeing the serving of the courses and their removes, Michael could barely take his eyes off Natalie. In the glow of the great branching silver candelabra on the dining room table and the sconces on the walls, she seemed to sparkle. Her cheeks were flushed, her lips slightly parted.

She was talking with that sports-mad fool, Lord Ashford. What could she possibly see in him that put such a light in her eyes? Michael's teeth ground together, quite without any volition on his part. He remembered Josef's mentioning casually a few nights before that Mr. Maximilian Chesney believed that the dowager countess and Lord Ashford would make a good match. The thought stung Michael.

Certainly, the young man was handsome enough, if you liked English sides of beef. He had reddish skin, thick blond hair, and handsome blue eyes, if you didn't mind the vacancy in them that dissipated only when he talked of foxhunting or the Fancy. And, of course, he was a viscount, with a sizeable estate in Dorset. Gossip in the servants' hall, however, said that the land was heavily mortgaged and that Lord Ashford would not be averse to a little ready money. Surely Natalie couldn't be considering marrying a fool like that for a piddling bit of land in Dorset, a man who probably only wanted her for the wealth she had inherited. The bile rose in Michael's throat at the very thought.

"Umm—er—Mr. Schmidt . . ." said a low, tentative voice at Michael's side.

He started, and turned to see Oliver regarding him in a confused fashion.

"We've cleared the first course, Mr. Schmidt. Should we serve the second?" His tone expressed surprise at his superior's inattention.

"Yes, yes, of course, Oliver."

The main dish of the second course was a large roast of beef from the Amesworth home farm, which he had previously sliced and laid upon a platter. Michael grabbed this, grateful for the distraction, and started serving.

Heavens, but Natalie was lovely. He stared at the triple strand of pearls that lay across her bosom, emphasizing the soft round slopes and valleys.

She looked up at him and smiled sweetly. "Thank you, Mr. Schmidt," she said in her soft, gentle voice.

She glanced at her plate, then quickly up again at him through downcast eyelashes. Sweet, merciful heaven, was he hallucinating? Surely that could not be invitation in her gaze. A lady did not make eyes at her butler like that. At least, not as proper a lady as Natalie Chesney, dowager Countess of Amesworth.

He gulped, and moved on hastily.

*   *   *

Michael sat up with a start, blinking. The dark room seemed strange and unfamiliar. This was not his suite in Stellberg's palace, its white and gilt painted paneling inset with mirrors. Still misty with sleep as he was, he surveyed the small, barren room in the streak of silver moonlight falling through the single uncurtained window. He remembered. He was not in Estavia any longer. This was England, where he was serving as a butler.

What had made him feel as if he were in Estavia again? He had dreamed . . . What had he been dreaming? There had been shouts, and the fire of torches winding through narrow streets. He rubbed his eyes, still hearing the shouts echoing in his ears. "Michael, Michael, Michael! Prince Michael! Michael for our reigning prince. No more Napoleon! Down with Carl Friedrich!"

He had gone out onto the balcony, he remembered, and remonstrated with the mob gathering in the street below. He would have no part in any plot to overthrow his brother, he had told them. But the mob had not listened. Instead, from where he stood, thirty feet above them, he had seen a wild, gathering frenzy pulsing through the crowd. One man, standing at the forefront of the mob, had raised his arm and thrown something, and Michael had heard the sound of shattering glass from one of the tall windows below his feet.

Michael shuddered. The dark, nightmarish quality of his dream still possessed him, as real and as vivid as it had been on the night it happened. He had withdrawn from the balcony, convinced there was no controlling the mob that night. He could have called out the army to disperse them, but he loathed the thought of the bloodshed that would result. His half brother was absent from the capital, so Michael took counsel with Carl Friedrich's most trusted advisor, Count Rittenauer. Between them they agreed that the only recourse was for Michael to leave the country temporarily, to allow the people the opportunity to calm down. Rittenauer promised that he would make every attempt to control the rioting populace and also to explain Michael's decision to Carl Friedrich.

Temporarily. Sitting in his attic room at Amesworth Court, Michael shook his head. It had been seven months since he had left Estavia, and still there was no answer but stony silence from Carl Friedrich. Michael had made one last attempt to clarify his position when he wrote to Carl Friedrich protesting Antonia's forthcoming marriage. That had been two months ago, shortly before he took this position as a butler, and still he had heard nothing.

Throwing off the bedclothes, Michael swung his feet to the floor. Nothing had changed in the situation regarding Carl Friedrich and Estavia. So why was he dreaming of it now?

Even as he asked himself the question, he knew the answer. Nothing had changed regarding Carl Friedrich and Estavia, but something *had* changed in Michael.

He recalled again—as he had all the previous day—the kiss that he and Natalie had shared the morning before. Her lips had been quite as satisfying as he had ever dreamed they would be. Now, in the privacy of his room, he remembered how soft and supple she had felt beneath his hands.

What was it about her that was so intriguing? He had known many women, starting with the jaded Hungarian countess he had met in Vienna when he was sixteen, who had found it amusing to initiate the young prince into the arts of love. He had learned a great deal.

From then on, a parade of lovely women had followed—from charming and voluptuous chambermaids who could not resist enticing a handsome prince to their beds to demure and not-so-demure young ladies from the courts of almost every German state, all of whom had thought that it would not be so bad to wed a prince, even if he did not stand in direct succession.

There had even been some talk of his marrying a young niece of the Austrian emperor, in order to cement Estavia's alliance to the empire. Michael had been glad when that failed, though, for the young lady had borne far too close a resemblance to her cousin Marie Louise, who had become the second empress of France. Michael supposed that he would not necessarily have noticed those bug eyes in bed, but Maria Amelia's vapid conversation had been extraordinarily hard to tolerate.

So why did little Natalie Chesney attract him so? Why did even the thought of her shy kisses—hesitant and eager at the same time—send his blood pulsing through his veins? She was lovely, true, but he doubted that she had stood out particularly in London Society. Still, her response to him went right to his heart. And then he realized the answer.

Natalie was responding to *him*, to plain "Michael Schmidt," her butler. Every other woman—even the Hungarian countess who had taken his virginity—had doubtless wanted him more avidly because he was a prince, because of the aura of his name and lineage. Natalie had no idea that he was anything other than far beneath her in rank. Yet still she had kissed him.

Sitting on his bed, he felt his body heat at that thought. If only . . .

No! He leapt up and crossed the drafty, bare boards to the basin of cold water on his washstand. Dashing the water on his face, he lectured himself. He had never lied to a woman he seduced before. He would not start now. Her response to him yesterday morning tempted him, but to initiate kisses or even more while she believed him merely a servant would be as much a lie as if he had led some chambermaid to believe he would marry her. He would not do it. He must not do it, no matter how strong he found the temptation.

Letting the cold water drip down his face and onto his chest, making his nightshirt cling clammily to him, he lectured his recalcitrant body firmly. He must revert immediately to the image of the perfect butler.

He groaned. Some things were simply too much to ask of a man. When he had first taken this position, he had thought of it as a larkish way of maintaining himself and his sister until Carl Friedrich summoned him back to Estavia. Well, enough was quite enough. He would leave his job here and return to Estavia without invitation. Surely, face-to-face with Carl Friedrich, they could reach a reconciliation. And, arguing in person, surely he could make Carl Friedrich see that Antonia must not undertake this Bonaparte alliance.

Tomorrow would come soon, and tomorrow he would resign.

Michael was overseeing the final preparations of the cold luncheon collation when Josef brushed by him with a large pile of freshly starched, snowy white cravats.

"Meet me in the laundry room when you're free," he muttered in Michael's ear as he passed.

Something in his tone of voice made Michael finish up his duties as quickly as he could, then repair posthaste to what had become their accustomed rendezvous site.

Josef was brushing one of Maximilian Chesney's coats, but he immediately laid down his brush and pulled a letter from his pocket.

It had been re-addressed from London, but Carl Friedrich's princely crest was clearly evident on the wrapper.

Michael bit his lip.

"He's written," he said. "At last."

"Yes," Josef replied.

Sitting down on his preferred perch on the windowsill, Michael slit the wrapper and pulled out the letter. He perused it in silence, then read it again. Finally he sat staring at it.

"I gather the news is not good," Josef said quietly.

Michael looked up. "My brother believes I am a traitor," he said bleakly. "He writes that I am not, under any circumstances, to return to Estavia. He also—not surprisingly, I suppose—writes that he is much disturbed by my attitude toward Antonia's betrothal to Orlando Bonaparte."

He looked out the window, seeing not the gently rolling parkland but rather a starker landscape, where great dark evergreens cloaked the German Alps in a perennial mystery.

"Carl Friedrich does not understand. Estavia is not his country alone. It is mine, as well," he muttered in a low voice. "It is not my fault that my countrymen love me. I have never had any designs on the crown. I do not know how Carl Friedrich can believe that I would. Yet here he says that he knows I plotted to usurp the throne, that the rebellion that night was at my behest. I don't understand. Carl Friedrich and I do not always agree, but he has never refused point-blank to hear me out before."

He laughed bitterly. "The irony, Josef, I had just decided last night to forfeit my pride and return to Estavia to throw myself upon Carl Friedrich's mercy."

Josef sat bolt upright. "You had decided *what?*"

"I am growing tired of this charade, Josef. Who knows who I may hurt before it's over? I hate the way I am deceiving the countess . . ."

Josef's face grew alert. "The countess?"

Michael felt himself flushing. "She is my employer, after all . . ."

"My prince, you have no choice but to remain. As you have said, you have compelling reasons. The princess, your sister, surely must be one of them."

Michael laughed. "Well, here's a turnaround. Weren't you the one who was insisting that I demeaned myself in such a role?"

"But now, my prince, when you have been here so long, you would be breaking your word—the honor of the house of Stell—if you were to resign and leave the countess without notice. In the middle of her house party, no less."

Michael waved the letter. "I don't think I have much choice, Josef. Carl Friedrich has spoken. I will be staying on for a few more weeks at least. But it won't be much longer than that. I think I must bury my pride completely and write to the Prince Regent for help."

He stood and folded the letter carefully, placing it in his pocket. Then, pasting a light-hearted grin to his face, he waved at Josef and left the room. Only when he had closed the door carefully behind him did he let the smile drop.

"Damn," he muttered under his breath. "Damnation. Carl Friedrich, you do have the most terrible timing."

Chapter Fourteen

*N*atalie was discovering that it was one thing to make a brave decision to finally become a woman of the world, and quite another to implement that decision when the object of her affections seemed unwilling to notice he had been chosen for that momentous event. Unchaperoned opportunities did not often appear.

Also, she had no idea how one went about initiating a liaison of the type she was imagining. In fact, she was coming to the conclusion that it was considerably harder than she had originally thought.

Necessity, however, finally came to her rescue. In the morning's post, she received a missive from the new earl and his wife, assuring her that they would be leaving Jamaica within the month, following hard on the heels of their communication. By the middle of August, at the latest, they would be in England.

Since it was already early August, it now became imperative that she complete her arrangements to move into the dower house. House party or no house party, she must repair to the dower house with a team of maids, along with footmen to do the heavy lifting, and oversee scrubbing the place from top to bottom. And if she were bringing the footmen, then perhaps she should bring along her butler to manage them.

And, she thought with a certain smug satisfaction that was most uncharacteristic, any enterprising lady should be able to find herself alone with her butler at some point during this endeavor. Once she found herself alone, how hard could it be to seduce a man, even one so apparently oblivious to her attractions as Michael Schmidt?

Tomorrow, she thought. *Tomorrow we will be alone together.*

And tonight she would lay some further groundwork. Smiling to herself, she directed Gwyneth to lay out her midnight blue silk dress and the sapphire and diamond necklace that complemented it so well.

Was it merely his overly heated imagination, Michael wondered, or did Natalie Chesney become more alluring with every passing day? She seemed to have completely abandoned the prim, virginal gowns in which she had attired herself when he first met her.

Tonight she was wearing a lustrous silk of deep blue, so soft and fine that he longed to run his hands across its smooth surface, tracing the curves that lay beneath.

He was learning, because he had no choice, how to act the part of the perfect butler when every inch of his body cried out to be kissing Natalie. She was pouring the evening tea right now, and he was passing around the delicate china teacups as she filled them. Standing motionless in front of her, waiting for the next cup, he could only hope that he kept his face impassive. He could not, however, prevent himself from watching her as she lifted the heavy silver teapot and directed a stream of tea into each cup.

This dress, like so many she had been wearing of late, was cut low, revealing the silky white upper curves of her breasts. Tonight she wore a delicate strand of sapphires and diamonds, with a single large sapphire nestling into the shadowed valley between her breasts.

He heard a discreet cough, designed to attract his attention, and realized to his horror that Natalie had finished pouring a cup and was waiting for him to serve it. She smiled at him.

He bent to take the full cup carefully from the table. As he straightened again, his eyes met hers, and he saw the tip of her pink tongue momentarily appear between her white teeth, moistening her lips in a gesture of attraction as old as woman.

The cup wavered in his hand, and the tea nearly spilled. By the time he retrieved it from disaster, Natalie's expression was neutral once again. He half thought he had imagined the episode, but she wore a look of secret satisfaction, as if his reaction had pleased her. He knew then that their impulsive kiss in the meadow had been both too little and too much. They could never retrieve the proscribed, restricted relationship of mistress and servant now. He should have left when he made his vow to do so, but he still felt bound by impossible circumstance.

The cup he held was the final one. He handed it to Lord Ashford, feeling particular pleasure in leaving him until last. The man did not deserve someone as enchanting as Natalie Chesney. Taking the tea tray from her, he carried it to a sideboard, where he stood at attention in case anything further was required.

The ladies had been demonstrating their skills upon the pianoforte that evening. Emily Seabury, who clearly loved music and was talented at it, had led the way with a lovely Beethoven sonata.

Natalie had then been prevailed upon to play, and the sight of her suitors clustering around her and turning pages for her had caused Michael to bring in the tea tray a full half hour early. Poricy was all very well, for it was hard to believe that any woman would spare him even a glance, but the way Lord Ashford lustfully peered down

Natalie's bosom angered Michael. How dare the man think the thoughts he so clearly was thinking? It was a disgrace.

Michael carefully avoided considering the direction of his own thoughts.

Currently Jane Hargrave was massacring Mozart. Michael winced as she pounded through yet another passage. Her keystrokes were scrupulously correct, and her timing was as regular as a metronome, but the effect on Mozart was worse than if she had played with enthusiasm and hit the occasional wrong note.

Michael could see a pained expression on his sister's face, too. Toni shared his love of music, and though she was not particularly talented on the pianoforte, she had a charming singing voice. He was glad to see that she was sitting across the room from Vincent Delamere, chatting brightly with the late earl's two elderly aunts.

Jane came to the end of one Mozart piece and appeared poised to start yet another.

Antonia jumped up from her seat. "Oh, Mrs. Hargrave," she implored, "do allow me to play now."

Jane frowned at her disapprovingly, and Michael acknowledged to himself that it would have been more strictly polite of his sister to wait until Jane Hargrave left the pianoforte of her own accord. But, really, it was a kindness to all in the room to spare their ears yet another wooden rendition.

"Oh, yes, Antonia," Natalie said enthusiastically. "We haven't heard you sing yet. I remember when we were at school together, you sang some charming folk songs from Estavia. Perhaps you could do so tonight."

Jane shrugged crossly and vacated the piano stool. She stalked over to her husband, talking with him in a low voice, and soon after both left the room.

"A folk song?" said Antonia. "Oh, that's a good idea,

Natalie. Let me think . . . which one?" A naughty light appeared in her eyes, and she giggled. "Oh, I know."

She tripped lightly over to the pianoforte. As she passed Michael, who was still standing by the sideboard, she whispered, "Listen closely to this."

Michael felt a shadow of apprehension. Toni clearly had something a trifle wicked planned, and there was nothing he could do about it.

The moment she played the first notes, he knew why she had looked so mischievous. Certain that only her brother would recognize it, and secure in the knowledge that he was the sole other person present who spoke German, she was playing a drinking song. Where in the world she had learned it was another matter. Their mother must be rotating in her grave.

He held his breath, for the song told a naughty story, the tale of a handsome lord out hunting and the pretty maid he met picking flowers in a meadow, with a chorus running, "Drink, drink, drink, my friends, and may we all be so lucky." Michael wondered if Toni even understood the implications. Toni finished four verses and stopped. Michael started breathing again. Clearly whoever had so improperly taught her the song had at least had the good sense to conceal the existence of the later verses in which the lord took the young peasant girl back to his castle to have his way with her. A kiss was all the pair shared in the version Toni knew.

He was going to have to give her another lecture, though, the next time he had the opportunity. It was most improper for her to have sung the song at all, and he would also like to ascertain why she had seen fit to direct it specifically at him. Surely, she hadn't noticed the unusual tension between himself and her friend.

*   *   *

Michael was overseeing the cleaning of the silver teapot, spoons, and serving tongs used for the tea when the upstairs bell rang. He sent Oliver up to see what was needed, and the young footman came back in a few minutes to report that the countess was doing accounts in the library and would like a cup of chocolate brought to her there.

Sighing, Michael sent Oliver in to the kitchen to direct the cook to prepare the hot chocolate. It was late, and he was hoping that the staff could retire soon. Most of the gentlemen guests were in the billiards room and showed no signs of seeking their bedchambers, but he had personally filled all the decanters and made sure to place extra wine and port in the sideboard. He had hoped that would preclude any more requests.

"I'll take the chocolate up, Oliver," he said. "I want this silver finished so I can put it away in the safe. With both you and Percy working on it, it should be nearly done by the time I return."

Putting the cup of chocolate on a tray, he carried it upstairs to the library, where Natalie was sitting at the big desk, wearing her gold-rimmed spectacles, which looked endearing with her low-cut evening gown.

She glanced up from the huge leather-bound accounts book. "Mr. Schmidt . . . Michael," she said, flushing. "I was expecting Oliver again." She took off the spectacles and placed them beside the ledger.

Michael set the tray down on the desk and turned to leave.

She quickly put a hand on his arm. "No . . . wait," she said. "Don't go. I have something . . ."

She faltered to a halt.

He waited patiently.

She flushed again. "I was wondering . . ." she began. "You could tell me, I've just realized . . . What was it that

Princess Antonia was singing tonight? She wouldn't tell me. She merely giggled when I asked her."

"It was most unsuitable," said Michael sternly.

"But what did it say? Tell me what the words would have been in English," she persisted.

He knew he shouldn't tell her. He knew he should simply turn and leave, but she was his employer, and she had given him a direct order. More to the point, however, she was also an irresistible woman.

She caught his hand in hers and pressed it against her cheek. "Please, Michael," she coaxed, "I'm longing to know. Tell me."

The feel of her soft skin against his hand was his downfall. She had no idea, of course, what she was doing to him, but he could not resist her.

"It's a drinking song," he said reluctantly. "A naughty tale of a noble lord and a young peasant girl." He hummed a few measures under his breath, remembering nights spent with the officers of his regiment, pounding their beer mugs on the table as they sang the chorus.

"How does it go?" she coaxed, her breath warm and gentle on his skin.

"'*Eine schone Madchen*,' that is, a pretty maid. A pretty maid goes out to a meadow in the woods one morning early in May. She's gathering flowers, you see, to celebrate the spring. A young baron out hunting in the woods rides by on his horse. He sees the pretty maid sitting in the meadow with the flowers in her lap, and he admires her beauty. Then comes the chorus . . ." He hesitated.

"Yes," Natalie prompted.

"The chorus is a little naughty. It goes 'Drink, drink, drink, my friends, and may we all be so lucky.'"

He saw that her big blue eyes were wide with bewilderment. "I don't understand," she said. "Why is that naughty?"

He hadn't realized she was such an innocent. "It's what happens later in the song," he said reluctantly.

"And what does happen then?"

He swallowed hard. He'd been hoping to avoid that part. "The baron takes the maiden off to his castle," he explained as sketchily as he could, "and the gentlemen singing the song are saying that they wish they could find as beautiful and . . . as compliant a lady."

"Oh," she said softly, her eyes revealing she now understood. Her lips were parted, and she was breathing a little fast.

She stood, and he could see her breasts heaving a bit above the deep blue silk. He stepped back a pace, putting distance between them, but she moved with him.

"It's a little like you and I in the meadow, then," she said softly. "Did the baron kiss this maiden as she sat in her meadow?"

He smiled involuntarily, thinking of the more explicit details of the later verses. "Uh, yes, he kissed her."

"And did she like it?"

"She seemed to," he conceded.

"I liked it," she said shyly.

She had moved even closer to him, until they were almost touching. His own breath was faster now, too.

"I liked it," she repeated. "I liked you kissing me, Michael. Would you do so again?"

He groaned, tempted beyond resistance, and bent his head to hers. Her mouth was warm and willing beneath his, as sweet and innocent as it had been the morning in the meadow. What a long way they had come since he had been reprimanded in this very room for kissing her hand—and how right she had been to do so. The temptation she offered was too sweet for him to resist.

He deepened the kiss. She faltered backward slightly,

and he raised his head and quickly steadied her with one strong arm about her waist.

They stood a long moment so, gazing at each other. Then there was a sound at the door, as if someone were fumbling at the handle.

They sprang apart, and Natalie hastily seated herself at the desk once again. The door handle moved up and down a few times, and finally the door opened. Horace Poricy stumbled through, and stood staring at them owlishly.

"Oh," he said thickly, "I thought—I thought thish wash the billiardsh room."

"This is the library, Mr. Poricy," said Natalie. "And I am working on my accounts just now."

"Sh-shorry, Countesh. I wash looking for the billiardsh room."

"You said that already, Mr. Poricy. I think perhaps you should be looking for your bedchamber. You have clearly drunk enough for the night." She turned to Michael. "Schmidt, find Mr. Poricy's valet and have him escort Mr. Poricy to his room."

"Sh-shouldn't be so drunk," confided Horace. "Don't usually drink sho much. But I'm worried about what that fellow at the inn might do. He'sh shtill hanging around, you know."

"No, I do not know," said Natalie briskly. "In fact, Schmidt, I think you should not delay. Would you please show Mr. Poricy the correct way to his room yourself? And make sure that if his valet is not already there that he attend him there soon."

Michael bowed. "Certainly, milady. I will do so." Taking a wobbling Horace Poricy by the arm, he guided him from the library.

As Poricy stumbled up the stairs, he looked anxiously at Michael. "Sh-shouldn't have shaid that. About the fellow at the inn. B-but maybe the countesh didn't notish. Good thing you're just the butler."

"Good thing," said Michael, thinking that the fellow at the inn was probably the last thing on either his or Natalie's mind at that moment.

The fact that he was just the butler, on the other hand, was definitely on his mind.

Chapter Fifteen

*W*hen morning came, Natalie had already jumped out of bed, humming a song, before she realized why she was so cheerful. The tune was the one Antonia had sung the night before. Natalie couldn't manage the unfamiliar German words, but she knew that forever after even a bar or two of the music would remind her of the way Michael had held and kissed her last night.

She was finally making progress in her attempted seduction, she thought in elation. After last night, she could have no question that he was attracted to her. And today she would at last have the chance to arrange for the privacy they needed. Perhaps it was fortunate that Horace Poricy had stumbled in when he did. The library would have been almost as uncomfortable a place to make love as the stone bench Alden had refused to consider. There was a very nice bed at the dower house with a brand-new feather mattress installed just last month.

"Is this the dress you were wishing to wear, milady?" asked Gwyneth from behind her.

Natalie turned and saw her maid holding out a simple day dress, a plain one quite suitable for overseeing the scheduled cleaning at the dower house.

"No," she said. "No, I've changed my mind, Gwyneth. I'll wear the figured muslin instead."

Even as she said the words, she wondered at herself. The figured muslin was not the most practical of dresses for a busy, dusty day. But it *was* the most attractive of her day dresses, she thought. And today, for once, she was going to be impractical.

Immediately following breakfast she initiated a flurry of scrubbing and dusting at the dower house. She felt exhilarated and channeled it all into the cleaning. It was shocking how dirty a place could become when it had not been attended to in fifteen years. Luckily, the house was small—only five bedrooms and a boudoir upstairs, and two withdrawing rooms and a dining room downstairs. She directed the maids to start at the top and work down, and by midday they were hard at work on the withdrawing rooms.

Natalie's stomach tightened. It was nearly time for the next stage of her plan. Surreptitiously she loosened her fichu a little from its usual demure folds.

"Where would you like these curtains, milady?" asked Michael from behind her.

Natalie turned from her contemplation of the shocking state of the drawing room carpet, the hollow feeling of excitement in the pit of her stomach threatening to overwhelm her.

Heavens, but he was good-looking. She longed for the freedom to run her hands through his dark, crisp hair.

First, however, she had to maneuver some privacy. Oliver and Percy were standing patiently behind him, yards of deep red brocade piled in their arms.

"We need those upstairs," she said briskly, leading the way. The excitement she had felt earlier was turning to nervousness in the reality of the moment. It had seemed easier at the planning stage.

She desperately hoped she knew what she was doing.

*   *   *

The dower house was a little jewel of a place, thought Michael as he helped Percy and Oliver hang the curtains in the windows of the main bedroom—a charming setting for a charming woman. It was hard on his resolve to ignore such charms, but he was determined not to allow his weakness to betray him again.

As they hung matching curtains around the great four-poster bed, however, he imagined her asleep in it, pure and virginal-looking in a snow-white chemise, her glorious red-gold curls spread out across her pillow. She was looking exceptionally pretty today, with a light flush across her cheekbones. He wondered whether she, too, was thinking of the previous evening.

"Wonderful," she said enthusiastically when the curtains were all hung. "Percy, Oliver, you have done very well. You may return to the main house now. Mr. Schmidt, I wish you to stay for a few moments to consult on one last matter."

She sat down at the old-fashioned escritoire and started to write some notes. He waited patiently, wondering what she wished to ask him. The door closed behind Percy and Oliver.

Natalie started—almost guiltily, it seemed—and a rosy flush swept across her face.

"Mr. Schmidt . . . M-M-Michael . . ." she stammered.

"Yes, milady?" he asked.

She stood up and walked toward the door. She seemed oddly nervous, and he wondered if she was now uncomfortable over the impropriety of their embrace the previous evening. Perhaps she was going to reprimand him for that, although he thought she had been the first to be forward.

"Yes, milady?" he asked again.

She reached the door and grasped the key that was in the lock, turning it so the bolt shot home.

"Milady!" he repeated, shocked.

She turned from the door with a strange look on her face, shy but defiant. He realized they were alone in a bedroom together.

"Did you . . . did you . . . like kissing me last night?" she asked, moving closer to him.

What an insane question! Of course he had liked it.

"You seemed to enjoy it," she continued.

"I . . . I . . . what . . ."

"Such a pity Mr. Poricy interrupted us."

"Well . . . well, yes, it was a pity," he admitted honestly.

"We won't be interrupted this time," she said.

He thought of the door she had just locked. "I suppose not," he responded, licking his lips, which were suddenly very dry.

She took one of his hands in both her own and placed his fingers on her breast. He could feel its soft rounded swell and his blood raced.

"I like how that feels," she said simply. "I liked it when you kissed me last night. I would like . . . I would like it if you were to . . . kiss me more."

The great four-poster bed was positioned invitingly behind her. She was asking to be kissed and touched. Did she have any idea what she was saying?

He lowered his mouth to cover hers. She was sweet, so sweet, her honeyed lips soft and pliant beneath him. She moaned under his touch.

Greatly daring, he cupped her warm, full breast.

She gasped, and instantly he released her, certain he must have caused offense, but she simply gazed up at him with wide, passion-glazed eyes. With one hesitant finger she caressed his cheek.

"That feels so wonderful," she murmured softly. "I had no idea. I wish I had known long ago. Will you . . . will you be my lover, Michael?" she asked haltingly.

Then she hurried on as if embarrassed but determined to speak her piece. "We can be discreet, and no one would ever suspect. My reputation will be safe. And of course, I will make sure you are . . . well-rewarded. I would not want to encourage a gentleman, because he would then expect me to marry him, and I do not want to be married. But you? There can be no thought of marriage between us. Will you teach me the joys of love, Michael?" She finished in a rush, blushing brilliantly.

Michael gasped. He felt as if a bucket of cold water had been thrown over him, effectively quenching his feverish passion. He wrenched himself away from her.

"What are you proposing, your ladyship?" he asked harshly. "A liaison with a servant? Are you truly willing to demean yourself so?"

He reached out and grasped her shoulders, fairly shaking her. "You think I'm safe, do you? I would have no thoughts of marriage—is that what you said? You could indulge your longing for a little passion, and then we could part and go our separate ways? Oh, yes, and you would 'reward' me. How much would you be willing to pay me to service you, milady?" he asked brutally, masking the hurt he felt.

He took a hard, shuddering breath, then realized that tears had gathered in her wide blue eyes and were running slowly down her cheeks. One part of him longed to hold and comfort her, but the insult he felt was too grave.

He bowed crisply. "I am, as always, your obedient *servant*, milady." Turning on his heel, he unlocked the door and left the room.

Natalie stood where he left her, too shaken to move. She had made a terrible miscalculation. Despite her belief that they could have a love affair, she *had* been guilty of considering him as a servant, not a man. How else could she, when all her upbringing had taught her that servants were treated so. But by doing so, she had insulted him beyond retrieval.

Unfortunately, in her heart, she knew it was as a man she loved him. And that, more than anything else, would erect an insurmountable barrier between them—one they would never overcome—for of course a lady could never marry a servant.

Chapter Sixteen

From past experience, Natalie knew the surest way to put troubles out of her head was to bury herself in work. She certainly had enough to occupy her. Not only was she hostess to a house party while simultaneously renovating the dower house, but she still had all the responsibilities that came with being a landowner.

"I have to visit some of my tenants today," she said one morning to Antonia. She and her young friend were enjoying a breakfast alone together, earlier than the other guests.

"May I come with you?" asked Antonia. "I feel in desperate need of fresh air. I would prefer to escape certain . . . attentions toward me."

"If you wish," Natalie replied with some doubt. "But I'm going over to End Farm, and I am planning to walk. It can be very muddy in the fields, even in the middle of summer."

"A little mud doesn't bother me," said Antonia firmly.

"Then I would be delighted for the company. I wonder whether Mrs. Simms will have her baby today," she added, almost to herself, as she thought about her responsibilities. "She's past due, now, and I promised I would bring dinner for her husband and children the day she does. She has seven already, so that is a lot of mouths to feed. She said she would send Tommy or one of the other children over when her time came."

Finishing off her slice of bread and butter and her tea, she stood up briskly. "Can you be ready within half an hour, Antonia?" she asked. "I need to be on my way."

Antonia signified that she could, and Natalie opened the door that led from the room. In the hall, she nearly bumped into Vincent Delamere, who was hanging about for no apparent reason. She passed him by with a polite word, then saw to her preparations for her morning without giving him a second thought. Toni was as good as her word, and within twenty minutes they had started out.

"I'm glad to see you took my warning about the mud and wore stout boots," Natalie remarked as the two climbed over the stile in the hedge that separated this side of the park from the farmland beyond. "Down here by the stream, where the cows come to drink, the ground is always very chopped up."

Antonia dimpled. "I may have spent far too many years in Bath, but I'm a country girl at heart, Natalie. I grew up running wild in the woods at Schloss Stell with my brother."

"Yes, that's right," said Natalie. She fell into silence, for the mention of Schloss Stell had reminded her of Michael and the disastrous mull she had made of her affairs. A discreet affair had seemed attractive, but she feared her feelings were already too deeply engaged to be appropriate in a relationship with a servant. And her distress over Michael's reaction indicated just how engaged her emotions were.

The two women navigated the mud by the little footbridge over the stream, then set off across the pasture. The grass was a brilliant green speckled with pale yellow cowslips, and the sun shone brightly. It was hard to stay dismal for long on such a day.

Antonia chattered nineteen to the dozen, as was her way, and Natalie found herself sinking into a reverie, soothed by the gentle flow of Toni's inconsequential observations on the weather, the house party, school, life, and anything else that entered her head.

"Have you ever been in love, Natalie?"

Startled, Natalie stopped and stared at Antonia. Unbidden, an image of Michael's lean, dark face rose in her mind. She felt her breath catch.

"Well . . . I'm sorry . . . perhaps I shouldn't have asked," Antonia stammered. "I just wondered . . . seeing as how you've been married . . . whether you had ever . . . Oh, I don't know! I don't think I'm saying this very well at all. But I'm going to be married, too, I'm afraid, to some man I've never met and know nothing about, and . . ."

"I loved my husband as a wife should do, Toni," said Natalie, but then she took pity on Antonia's misery. "I don't think that is what you are trying to ask, however. Romantically, with a young man your own age? Is that what you want to know?"

Toni nodded.

"Yes, there was a man I loved once, when I was your age. I loved him very deeply."

"Then why didn't you marry *him?*" Antonia asked, wide-eyed.

"He died," Natalie said. She waited for the familiar deluge of sorrow to incapacitate her at the memory. To her surprise, it did not come. It seemed to have diminished. Finally, losing Giles had become a part of her youth, which she could now put aside.

She even found herself able to smile at Antonia's tragic expression. "It was a long time ago, my dear," she said, giving Toni a hug. "Right after I left the school in Bath. You were just a little girl. And then later, of course, I married Alden."

"But you weren't in love with him?" Antonia asked.

"I was very fond of him, but I never really had the

chance to fall *in* love with him, not as a woman does with a man," Natalie said slowly. She thought—against her will—of the pounding sweep of passion she felt when Michael kissed her.

"I loved Alden as a girl would love an older brother or her father," she said, carefully choosing her words. "He became ill too soon for me to ever feel any differently."

"But, I was wondering . . ." Antonia said hesitantly, "how do you know when you're in love? I mean, I thought I wanted Vincent to kiss me, but then, when he did, it was really rather nasty. I didn't like it much at all."

Natalie thought of how she had reacted to Michael's kisses. She had longed for more.

"I think," she said, "that if you truly loved a man, you would like it when he kissed you."

So if you wanted a man to kiss you, wanted it so much that your body burned with passion when he was not even anywhere near, what did that mean?

She closed her eyes, seeing again Michael's face as he gently placed his lips over hers, feeling once more the wonder of their warmth.

"Lady Amesworth! Princess Antonia!" A cry sounded from beyond the hedge that bordered the field. Natalie's eyes flew open.

To her surprise, she saw Vincent Delamere, in his high-perch phaeton, peering over the hedge.

"Lady Amesworth, thank heaven I found you. There's trouble with Mrs. Simms, a problem with her baby. She sent little Tommy over to the house. She needs you to come immediately. I said I would find you and escort you there."

"Mercy," said Natalie, her mind reeling at the barrage of information. "Do you know what happened? Is the midwife there?"

"I don't know. I just know she is asking for you urgently. Come along, then. I saw a stile about fifty feet back. I can drive you to her farm and then take the princess back to Amesworth."

"Well, it's definitely too far to walk from here," Natalie said, considering her options. She hated sporting vehicles—her parents had died in one—and she'd also seen the way Mr. Delamere drove his. "I'll hurry back to the house myself and have Hughes to take me in the landaulet."

"That will take too long," Delamere said urgently. "The child was very insistent that you come immediately. It will be much faster if I drive you."

"I suppose you're correct about that," she conceded reluctantly. "All right, I'll ride with you."

When they reached the break in the hedge, Delamere's groom jumped down and helped them over the stile, then up the high step into the perch phaeton. It was a difficult climb in skirts, and Natalie felt very vulnerable and exposed when she was finally perched on the high seat.

As soon as the two women were settled, Delamere cracked his whip with a flourish. Natalie clutched the seat with one nervous hand and looked warily at Delamere.

"Please, don't drive *too* fast," she said with a great deal of trepidation, for he truly was a reckless driver. She wished there were some other way, but the news from Mrs. Simms was too disturbing. The woman was usually so cool and calm; this was a strange departure for her. With seven youngsters already, she had given the impression that she considered childbirth very easy and natural. Natalie hoped desperately that the baby had not died.

Luckily, Delamere heeded her words, and kept the horses to a sedate trot. Even so, Natalie was sick to her stomach by the time they arrived at the farmhouse, a small but prosperous affair built of solid Cotswold stone.

"You can leave me here," she said, climbing down from the phaeton with relief, hoping she didn't look as green as she felt.

"As soon as you've taken the princess back to Amesworth, please ask Hughes to send a carriage for me," she said briskly. Now that she had both feet back on solid ground, she felt her usual, efficient self again. She didn't relish leaving Toni with Mr. Delamere for even the brief ride back to Amesworth, but it was an open carriage, so no impropriety could occur there. And she didn't want to risk having the girl come inside. If either the baby or the mother were dead or dying, it would be a difficult experience for the sheltered young Antonia to face.

Without waiting to wave good-bye, she hastened into the farmhouse. Two small boys were wrestling cheerfully on the kitchen floor, and a little girl was rocking a dolly. An older girl was stirring a pot of stew and Mrs. Simms herself was sitting calmly by the fireplace, sipping a mug of tea, her swollen ankles up on a settle in front of her.

"Your ladyship," she said in surprise. "How good of you to stop by. But as you can see, the wee babe still shows no sign of coming. Not so wee, actually. I think it's quite time he put in an appearance. He's bothering me night and day with his kicking, but drop down into place he will not do."

"You've not had any trouble?" Natalie asked.

"Nay, not a whiff of it. I don't expect none, neither. You mark my words. He'll slip out just as easy as his brothers and sisters did."

"You're convinced it's a boy, then?" Natalie asked.

"Well, he carries like a boy. I expect he will be."

"I'm glad to find you well, but it's strange," Natalie said carefully. "I received a message that there was trouble here. Did you send Tommy over to the Court with a message?"

"Me? Nay. Tommy and his dad have been out in the back field all day. I just saw Tommy five minutes past, when he came in to get a bite to eat for the two of them, so I know there's been no trouble out there, either."

"How odd," said Natalie. "One of my houseguests passed along the message. He must have been mistaken in some way. But I can't think how."

"Well, there's certainly naught wrong here. It was right good of your ladyship to drop everything and come, though. I do appreciate it. But you might as well be getting yourself home, unless you'd like to stay for a bite of something. Annie here could fix it quick as a wink."

"Well, I can't leave just yet," Natalie confessed. "Mr. Delamere, the gentleman who brought the message, dropped me off and took another lady home. I sent word for a carriage to fetch me, but that will take half an hour or so."

"Annie, make up a fresh pot of tea, girl. And there's some of my ginger cake in the larder. Get that out, too. We've bread and cheese, too, milady, if you're feeling peckish at all, though I don't have much else at this time of day, I'm afraid."

"No, no, that will be fine. The tea and ginger cake sounds lovely, Mrs. Simms. Are you knitting that shawl for the new baby?"

Mrs. Simms lifted her handiwork from her lap proudly. "I don't need much new, of course, because I have all the clothes from the older children. I do think a wee one should have one new thing for itself, however. I've always knitted a little something for each."

The conversation on babies continued over tea and ginger cake until the clock on the mantelpiece struck one.

Natalie jumped. "Heavens, it can't be one o'clock already. I've been here at least an hour. Where can the carriage from Amesworth be?" She looked over at Mrs. Simms. "Mrs. Simms, I hate to interrupt the farm work, but could Tommy or your husband take me home in your gig?"

"I'll have to get Tommy in from the fields, milady, but I'll send one of the children out for him right now. Bessie, sweetheart, put your dolly down and run to find Dad and

Tommy. Tell Tommy I need him. And tell Nate and Matt to stop scaring the chickens with their roughhousing in the yard and get in here."

In a few minutes, two freckle-faced boys shame-facedly poked their heads into the kitchen.

"I could hear you out there," their mother scolded them. "Now you two can make yourselves useful. Run and harness Blossom to the gig. Tommy's going to take her ladyship home."

Within ten minutes, the hulking, fifteen-year-old Tommy Simms was driving Natalie in the gig down the farm lane. Looking over at him, Natalie realized what had been teasing at the corners of her mind. Vincent De-lamere had referred to him as "little Tommy," but nobody would ever have called this overgrown lad little. Of course, it was entirely possible that Delamere had not ac-tually seen the lad, who would have come to the servant's entrance, but then why had Delamere acted as if he had seen Tommy when he came? If he had come at all . . . which now seemed unlikely.

Arriving back at the Court, she jumped down from the gig with a smile and a word of thanks for Tommy. She hastened up the front steps, feeling a concern that she hoped was out of proportion with the circumstances.

Michael opened the door himself. "Princess Antonia and Mr. Delamere must have returned an age ago," she said, trying to convince herself. "Can you tell me where Mr. Delamere is? I would like to speak with him."

She thought she saw a flash of concern cross her but-ler's face. "Mr. Delamere went out in his phaeton earlier this morning, milady. But the princess was with *you*."

"No, no. A problem arose. Mr. Delamere dropped me at the Simms farm and said he would bring the princess back to the Court. They must surely have returned an age past. I was delayed considerably."

There was no mistaking Michael Schmidt's concern. "We have not seen Mr. Delamere since he took his phaeton out shortly after you left, milady. Nor has the princess returned."

Natalie tensed, her distress escalating at this news. "Something is wrong. I am certain of it. Perhaps there has been an accident, though surely I would have seen them on the road if that had been the case."

Without waiting for her permission to leave, Michael spun on his heel. "I am going to speak to Delamere's man, milady," he said over his shoulder.

Left alone in the hall, Natalie felt uncertain what to do. The uncomfortable feeling that had hung over her all the way back from the Simms farm had intensified. Walking into the small parlor, she found Max sitting and reading a newspaper.

He jumped up, concern on his face. "Natalie, you look quite overset, my dear. Do sit down. Has something occurred to distress you?"

Unresisting, Natalie sat down. She gave a small, uncertain laugh. "I don't know," she confessed.

Max chafed her hands gently. "Where is Princess Antonia?" he asked. "You were out walking with her."

"I'm not quite sure where she is," Natalie replied faintly.

"But you left the house with her," Max said in surprise.

The door to the parlor swung open. Michael Schmidt stepped in, closing the door with a bang behind him.

Natalie stared at him, for his face was a tense, white mask of rage. She jumped up. "Michael, what is it?" she asked anxiously.

"Vincent Delamere's man says that Delamere is on his way to Gretna Green," he said coldly. "He told him that he would be gone several nights and to pack accordingly."

"No!" Natalie cried. "Oh, no, I can't believe that . . . Antonia would never . . . I can't believe . . ." She thought back to her earlier conversation with Antonia. She was convinced the girl had been saying she wasn't in love with Vincent Delamere.

"No, she wouldn't do that. She's been kidnaped," Michael said.

Natalie pressed her hands to her lips. "I'm afraid you may be right," she admitted.

Now that she had a few real facts, Natalie knew what she had to do.

"I must fetch her back," she said. "Max, please send a message down to the stables for a carriage. You and I must go after her so that I can chaperone her on her return. I can't possibly ask Lucretia to accompany me in her state of health, and nobody outside our family must know of this."

Max looked rattled, but he stood immediately. "Of course, my dear. It had better be the post chaise, I suppose."

"Yes, I think that's better than the landaulet," said Natalie. "We will have to go some distance, I'm afraid, and we certainly need to make haste. Tell them we need the post chaise, then, Max."

"No."

The single word came from Michael Schmidt.

Natalie swung around to stare at him incredulously.

"No," he repeated. "Even a post chaise will be too slow to catch Delamere's phaeton. I know you still have Lord Amesworth's curricle. I've seen the grooms take the horses out with it. If you will come with me, milady, to act as chaperone for the princess on the journey home, I can vouch that we will catch up with them before nightfall."

Natalie considered what he had said. "Yes," she said slowly. "Yes, I think you are right."

"I know I am right."

"But, Natalie," Max protested, "you don't like riding

in sporting vehicles. You never once allowed Alden to take you out in the curricle when he was courting you."

"Well, I don't like them," Natalie confessed, thinking of how frightened she had been in Delamere's phaeton, and that had been a brief, ten-minute journey accomplished at a slow trot. "But I don't see that I have much choice. Schmidt is right, Max, it's the only way that we can catch up with them today, before the princess is hopelessly compromised. I'm just going to have to steel myself to ride in the curricle. Now, we have no time to waste discussing this. Let me think what needs to be done. Max, you must tell the house party . . ."

She paused and thought. "Tell them that Princess Antonia and I decided on the spur of the moment to spend the day in Bath shopping. Of course, I would never really be so terribly rude, but that excuse is just going to have to suffice. I rely on your overly fertile imagination, Max, to supply any additional details that are needed."

She turned to Michael again. "Schmidt, I need to change my dress. I'll join you in the stable yard. We're less likely to be seen if you don't bring the horses around to the front."

She thought she saw a look of admiration on Michael's face, but all he said was, "Yes, milady. How long will you need?"

"No more than fifteen minutes," she said crisply. "It will take that long to get the horses and curricle ready. Tell Hughes fifteen minutes."

"Yes, your ladyship." He turned on his heel and left.

"Natalie," said Max urgently, "are you certain this is a good idea? At the very least, let me drive you."

Natalie patted him on the shoulder. "Max, my dearest, you're very kind to offer, but you hate sporting vehicles almost as much as I do. Have you ever actually driven one?"

"Once," Max admitted. "And I nearly got run away with. I've not done it again. But I would, Natalie, for you."

Natalie hugged him. "Cousin Max, you are a very dear person to offer," she said, kissing him on the cheek. "But I think it's better if we let Schmidt drive. He is clearly very confident of his own skills. For Antonia's sake, I must go with him."

"I still don't like it, Natalie," Max protested.

"I know what I'm doing, Max," Natalie replied, wondering a little at her own confidence. It was insane, and the thought of stepping into a sporting carriage for the second time that day made her sick with fear. Yet a still, certain center of calm within her told her that she was doing the right thing, that Michael Schmidt did know what he was doing, and she could trust him.

"Max, I'm afraid there's no time to be wasted," she said. "I must change. Can I trust you to make sure that nobody knows what is really happening?"

"Yes, but——"

Leaving him no further chance to object, Natalie swept from the room.

She nearly hit her cousin Jane on the nose with the door as she flung it open.

"Jane!" she exclaimed, "What are you doing here?"

Jane flushed slightly and opened her mouth to respond, but Natalie forestalled her.

"Don't bother to explain," she said. "I see you're still up to your old tricks. You got me into trouble quite a few times by listening at doors, didn't you?"

"You got yourself into trouble, Natalie," Jane responded righteously. "Just as you're doing at this very minute. I can't believe you would attempt such a thing, rescuing that little hussy. She deserves to see her reputation in shreds."

Natalie looked Jane up and down, feeling familiar anger rising within her. She didn't care what Jane thought or had to say. "I gather you heard every word, then," she said scathingly. "But how did you avoid being seen by Mr. Schmidt?"

"He was in too much of a hurry to notice me."

"You hid, did you?" speculated Natalie. "Such unbecoming behavior on your part, Jane. But how very like you."

"How dare you criticize me?" Jane screeched. "You're the one who is ruining the reputation of our family by running off with a butler. You will be driving through the countryside in an open carriage for the whole world to see. I am humiliated, Natalie. I will not have it."

"*You* will not have it," Natalie repeated. "*You* will not have it! To be quite frank, Jane, I don't care. You are my cousin, not my parent or husband. And at this moment, *my* concern is to see my friend rescued from an unpleasant situation as quickly as possible. Now, if you will excuse me, I am in a great hurry, and I'd appreciate your not detaining me."

Jane's mouth opened and shut several times, but no words came out. "Well," she said finally, "I have been grossly insulted. I am not staying in this house another minute. As soon as I can find Raymond, we will be leaving."

She began to stalk away, then turned back with a sly, triumphant smile. "What a tale I will have to tell, though. Society will be agog to hear the story."

Natalie was still sustained by her anger. Even this threat failed to deter her. "I don't think tittle-tattling would be very wise, Jane," she said coldly. "I think you forget that I know a few small details about you. Do you remember how you humiliated yourself when you were convinced that the Duke of Harcourt was proposing to you?"

Jane paled. "Natalie, you wouldn't . . . You never have said anything before."

"No, I never have, because I have too much common decency to do anything of the sort, even to you, Jane. But don't you think your precious Society would snicker to know that you were preparing to accept an offer of marriage from a man who was only asking you to dance, and that because his mother said he should? Sharp-tongued, mean-spirited Jane Thorpe, who required five years to find a man to marry her. If you drive me to it, Jane, I will tell everyone we know, if I have to make a special trip to London to do so."

The hatred in Jane's face was unmistakable. "I never did like you, Natalie," she said.

"You have made that abundantly clear for years, Jane. How nice that we now have it all out in the open."

"You won't be seeing me on your return from your injudicious expedition."

"I have no wish to do so, Jane. But I expect you to keep your mouth closed about this matter, or I will be forced to speak as well."

"All right, Natalie," said Jane sullenly, "you win this time. But just you wait."

"Good-bye, Jane," said Natalie, sweeping by her to the staircase, feeling a sense of triumph such as she had seldom experienced before.

Chapter Seventeen

*N*atalie did not allow either the discussion with Max or the contretemps with Jane to postpone her departure. Fifteen minutes after Michael left for the stables, she hurried down the stairs, pulling on stout leather gloves. She was wearing a serviceable woolen pelisse and a bonnet that fit closely and would not come off in the wind. Heaven only knew how long they would be on the road, and while the weather might be good now, there was no guarantee of its staying that way.

When she stepped out into the stable yard, Michael was already there, the curricle ready to go. Natalie stopped dead, feeling ill. He had not two but four of Alden's most treasured horses harnessed to it. Before the stroke that felled him, Alden had been one of the leading lights of the Four in Hand Club and regularly drove the curricle with these same four horses. He had always contended, however, that it was an extremely tricky operation with spirited blood horses like his, and she knew how true that was.

Natalie clenched her jaw. She had prepared herself for the need to ride in the curricle, but seeing the four horses unnerved her. Her father had been driving a team like this one the day that he had crashed his curricle and killed both himself and her mother. Until this day, when she had ridden in Delamere's phaeton, Natalie had never set foot in a sporting carriage. And Delamere had been driving only two horses, traveling a short distance at a sedate trot. Natalie could see in Michael's eyes that he had no intention of being sedate.

The horses were fidgeting, clearly itching to run. Michael turned to her. "Are you ready to leave, milady?"

She swallowed hard and nodded.

He spoke a word to the groom standing at the horses' heads, then climbed into the curricle. Another groom came running forward and helped Natalie into the other side. The horses shifted eagerly, and Michael steadied them with a practiced hand. They quieted, clearly recognizing the touch of a master.

Natalie clutched the side of the carriage. Her hands felt clammy, but she struggled to contain her anxiety. There was no need for any fear, she scolded herself. When Michael calmed the horses, she had recognized in that apparently simple movement the signs of skill. Years before, her father had taught her the signs of an experienced driver, and Michael clearly qualified.

With Alden's four prime goers to drive, Michael might actually catch up with Delamere, despite his nearly two-hour lead. Delamere was neither such a talented driver as he fancied himself, nor were his horses particularly fine stock, since he lacked the wherewithal to buy the best. Natalie knew they had a chance of rescuing her friend unscathed, but only if she mastered her fear.

"Are you ready?" asked Michael curtly.

"Yes," she said through tight lips.

He released the reins slightly and let the horses move forward through the arch that led from the stable yard. "Hold on," he said when they reached the drive. "I'm going to spring them."

"I am holding on," Natalie muttered, then gasped as he

let the anxious horses surge forward. The force of the acceleration pushed her backward into the seat, and she could see the trees of the park rush by.

He glanced over at her briefly. "All right?" he asked.

She nodded grimly.

"Then I'm going to let them out all the way. The road is nicely flat and smooth here in the park."

She smiled faintly. "I thought you were already springing them," she managed to say before they accelerated again.

She hung on to the front of the seat with one hand and to the side with her other, and braced her feet against the floorboards, closing her eyes for a second against the dizzying whirl. She opened them in time to see Michael gather up the horses with a practiced hand and steady them as he negotiated the bridge at the end of the lake.

He looked over at her, and for a moment his grim countenance relaxed. "I do a better job than Delamere, don't you think?"

She smiled at him tentatively. Despite her fear, she was finding the sensation of speed exhilarating. When she was a child, her father had often taken her out in his curricle, and she had forgotten how exciting the feel of the wind on her cheeks could be.

"You are an excellent driver," she said. He *was* a good driver—better than her father. Her father had taken unnecessary risks, such as the one that killed him and her mother. Already she could see that Michael didn't feel the need to prove anything by taking risks. "If we can just find which way Delamere has gone, I think we will catch up with him," she added.

"If he's really going to Gretna, he doesn't have many choices. And I believe he *is* going to Gretna. He'd be a fool to plan anything other than marriage with a princess."

They had reached the end of the park and were turning out into the village street. Michael was forced to slow for assorted children and dogs, as well as a wagon carrying vegetables. As soon as they left the village and headed toward the main post road, however, he let the horses out again.

It was tricky driving here, for the lanes were narrow and twisting, set deep with banks and hedges towering above them. The slightest miscalculation, and the carriage would be overset. Natalie sat quietly, because she knew he needed to concentrate, and she gripped the seat until her knuckles were white. She longed to ask him to slow down but knew their only hope of catching Delamere was to set such a pace. All she could do was trust Michael not to overturn them. And she did trust him. Otherwise, she'd be screaming with terror by now.

When they reached the comparative safety of the wide, straight post road that ran along the Ridgeline north toward Gloucester and Worcester, Natalie slowly started to relax. After a while, she discovered that she was actually enjoying herself. How liberating it was, after all these years of fear, to be able at last to shed it.

Michael remained quiet, concentrating on his driving, but she found herself sneaking glances at his handsome face, set in hard lines as it was. His muscled arms and long, fine hands were almost still, not disturbing the horses with unnecessary motion. Then, one of the leaders stumbled slightly, and she saw the power flowing through the sinews of Michael's forearms and hands as he encouraged the horse and gave it the balance it needed.

They were beautiful hands, she thought. Beautiful now, with tension evident in every line, giving them form and definition. And beautiful when he had touched her, soft and gentle as they had been then. The thought of his hands on her set her whole body humming in response.

At that moment she knew the truth, and knew as well that she had been a crazy fool not to see it before.

What a nitwit you have been, she scolded herself. *How could you have ever believed that what you felt for this man was mere physical passion?*

For years now, she had prided herself on her practical common sense. Now, out of the blue, she had allowed herself to be overcome by irrational emotion. She had fallen in love with a man she knew almost nothing about, and what little she did know made the thought of marrying him completely unthinkable. A lady did not marry her butler. She stared at him, feeling her heart rising in her throat.

As if he felt her eyes on him, he slowed the horses to a trot and glanced at her. "They're tiring," he said. "We're going to have to change them soon. Do you know where there's a posting stop?"

"We'll be in Stroud soon," she choked out. "I believe Alden used to do his first change there."

He looked at her more fully and must have seen in her face something of what she was thinking, for he slowed the horses to a walk. Wearied as they were, the high-strung beasts were now willing to move leisurely, with the reins hanging loose.

"Natalie," he said simply. It was just her name, yet the way he spoke it conveyed far, far more. He, too, felt a connection binding them. Was he willing to put behind him that episode in the dower house? Certainly she regretted it deeply and wished she could make him understand the depth of her remorse. They could have no future together, of course, but she did not want them to part in bitterness.

"Michael, I'm sorry I—"

"Hush," he said. "This is not the time. Let us have no regrets right now."

He cast an assessing look at the tired horses, then pulled them to a halt, letting the reins drop to his knees. Reaching over, he gathered her into his arms. Her whole body thrilled in response.

"I never dreamed," he said quietly, "of a woman like you. Never has a woman, from peasant to princess, moved my heart as you can with a single look."

She sighed and felt his arms tighten round her. "Natalie," he whispered again, and lowered his lips over hers in a kiss as gentle as it was masterful.

One of the horses shifted, and Michael reluctantly released her. His eyes were stormy and regretful as he said softly, "We have no time right now."

"I know," she replied. "We must find Antonia."

He pulled a gold watch with a crest she could not distinguish from his pocket, then slid it back. "It's past four already."

"Not quite five hours until dark then," she said. "We must ask after them in Stroud when we change the horses."

Two hours later they were sure they were on the right trail, for a young couple answering to Antonia's and Delamere's description had definitely been seen both in Stroud and in Gloucester.

"It's encouraging," said Michael, "that we are clearly gaining on them. Delamere is not the whip he believes he is."

"And you are one of the finest drivers I have ever met, and I met many as a child," said Natalie.

He shrugged his shoulders, concentrating on the road in front of him. Driving with tired horses required careful nursing and attention.

Natalie wondered where he had learned such a skill. From the beginning, he had struck her as an unusual example of a man in his supposed position. What they had shared today caused her to question his background. However, in their strange complicity as they pursued Antonia, they seemed to have arrived at an unspoken understanding that no questions would be asked.

"We're no more than an hour behind them now," Michael said.

"An hour?" Natalie echoed. "We were less than two hours behind them at the start. We'll never catch up with them by nightfall."

"We can only do the best we can," he replied calmly. He glanced around him. "This must be Tewkesbury we're coming into now. I see the coaching inn ahead."

While Michael questioned the grooms who ran out from the inn's stable, Natalie accepted the aid of one and slid gratefully down from the carriage. A curricle could be excruciatingly uncomfortable when one was a passenger for hour after hour. She walked slowly toward the inn, feeling the muscles in her thighs complain with stiffness and attempting to ease the cramp in hands that had ceaselessly gripped the edge of the seat. She was also in most urgent need of a place to relieve herself.

Once she had been shown to a private parlor, she inquired of the maid who brought a chamber pot about a young couple who might have passed through.

The maid smiled brightly. "Oh, yes, ma'am, they're here all right. Leastwise, if you're talking about a gentleman in a green coat with many capes, and a pretty young lady with green eyes and black hair. They're in the other parlor. I waited on them myself."

"They are the ones," said Natalie, barely able to contain her excitement. "Thank you, my dear."

She barely restrained herself from running out to shout the news to Michael. For the sake of Antonia's reputation, discretion was paramount.

She took the time to wash her hands and face and brush her windswept curls, then walked calmly down the stairs. Michael was striding purposefully into the inn toward her. "They're here," she said in a low voice.

"I know," he replied. "I've just seen Delamere's phaeton in the stable."

The innkeeper verified that the young couple were indeed upstairs in the second private parlor, and had been for over an hour.

Michael's face grew dark with rage. "What in damnation have they been doing there for an hour?" he growled.

Natalie clung to his arm. "Michael," she said in a low voice, "remember that we are not alone."

He shrugged her off and strode upstairs to pound thunderously on the door to the private parlor. Natalie followed at a more sedate pace, though she felt just as impatient herself.

Arriving at Michael's side, she found him scowling at the closed door.

"It's too quiet in there," he said. "What can that villain be doing with my—" He broke off. "There's no help for it. I'm going to have to break down the door."

"Michael," whispered Natalie in an agonized undertone, "we can't make such a scene. The whole inn will know."

"I can't leave Antonia alone in there with such a blackguard."

"Have you tried the door to see if it is locked?"

Michael grimaced. "No," he admitted.

"I think it would be a good place to start," said the ever-practical Natalie. Seizing the door handle, she found it turned easily under her hand.

Brushing her aside, Michael charged into the room ahead of her, then stopped in confusion.

Peering around him, Natalie saw a sunlit parlor with

white walls and dark oak beams, decorated in a pretty chintz. The room also appeared to be empty.

"They've left already!" Michael hissed.

There was something unusual about the room, Natalie felt, then realized she could see a broken vase and flowers strewn across the floor by the side of a settle that faced the fire.

She laid a hand on Michael's arm. "What's that?" she asked, pointing.

"A broken vase," he said crossly. "Come on, they must have sneaked out. We have to be on our way."

"No," said Natalie. "I want to see what's going on here."

She walked across the room. From her new angle, she could see a booted foot sticking out past the settle.

"Michael," she called, "come here."

They rounded the settle and found Vincent Delamere lying on the floor by the fireplace.

Natalie clutched Michael's hand. "Is he dead?" she asked.

He kneeled beside Delamere's body and slipped a hand into his coat. "His heart is still beating, and he's breathing," he announced.

Natalie sighed. "Well, that's a relief," she said. She looked at the tableau of body and vase again, and said, "You know, I have the strangest feeling that Antonia has rescued herself somehow."

She, too, kneeled down beside Delamere and looked closely at his brow. "There's a big knot here," she said. "I think Antonia may have hit him with the vase."

Michael surprised her with a crack of laughter. "Toni has never had much patience with people who attempt to force her to do things she doesn't wish to do," he said.

Natalie hadn't realized Michael knew Antonia so very well. She wondered briefly about it, but more important concerns intruded. "But where is she now?"

Michael laughed again. "Probably on her way back to Amesworth Court already. She won't be sitting around waiting to be rescued, that you can be sure of."

Natalie stood. "Well, then, what are we waiting for?" she said briskly. "We need to find Antonia."

Chapter Eighteen

*W*ithin half an hour, they were on the road back to Abbingford Magna. Rather to Michael's annoyance, Natalie had left money with the innkeeper to call a doctor for Delamere. On the bridge out of Tewkesbury, they found a small boy fishing, who had seen a pretty young lady with black hair walking briskly south along the post road.

"Heading home," said Michael. "But why didn't we see her?"

"It is peculiar," Natalie agreed.

A few miles north of Gloucester, however, they met another small boy with little to do that day. This one had seen a pretty lady descend from a wagon full of cabbages, which had been turning off in another direction. He was able to describe her dress as being blue, which was what Antonia had been wearing at the start of the day.

"I think we did pass a wagon of cabbages when we were headed north," Michael said. "I remember having to slow the horses as we went by."

"I wish I'd looked more closely," said Natalie, "but I was looking only for Delamere's curricle." *And at you*, she added silently.

They continued on in silence. With her anxiety about Antonia somewhat relieved, Natalie felt a new worry enveloping her. Today she had upset Max, mortally offended Jane, and crowned it all by running away in a curricle with her butler. All those concerns, however, paled in the face of her realization that she had fallen in love.

How in the world had it happened? She didn't want to be in love. She didn't want to feel such powerful emotions, with all the risks to her heart they entailed. She had her life nicely plotted out—a genteel and happy retirement in the dower house, puttering around her garden and visiting with her neighbors. She had no wish to be in love with anybody. Not with London's most eligible bachelor, and certainly not with this strange, enigmatic man sitting beside her. Exactly who was he, anyway? His behavior today had not resembled that of any butler she had ever met, and she no longer was willing to believe that his attitude toward Antonia was consistent with the concern of a family servant.

She glanced at Michael sideways, trying not to betray that she was looking. His face was shuttered. *What are you thinking now, Michael?* she wondered.

The silence was growing unbearable, the tension between them so heavy that she could feel its weight. She wished he would say something.

"Michael, we must talk," she said finally.

"I suppose we must," he said. She could hear the marked reluctance in his voice. Was he hiding some terrible secret?

"I—" she said.

"I have something that I must tell—" he said.

They both broke off, each realizing that the other was trying to speak.

"You were saying?" Michael said politely.

At that moment, she spotted a sudden scuffle in the hedge edging the road. She looked around, and saw a flash of blue.

"Michael!" she said urgently. "Michael, look there!"

He reined the horses in sharply. "What? Where?"

"Michael? Natalie?" called a quavering voice.

Michael pulled the horses to a halt. Natalie clambered down from the carriage as fast as she could in her hampering skirts.

"Antonia?" she called, running back along the road. "Antonia, darling!"

Bedraggled and rumpled, Antonia emerged from the hedge and fell into Natalie's arms. "Nini, Nini, you can have no idea how glad I am to see you. It has been the most terrible day!" She broke into tears.

"Hush, hush," Natalie soothed. "Everything is all right now. You're safe. We will take you home."

With an arm around the weeping girl, she walked her toward the carriage, then helped her climb in. Three on the seat of the curricle was a tight squeeze, but they managed.

Antonia turned toward Michael. "Michael, oh, Michael, thank you for coming to find me! I knew you would."

Holding the reins in one hand, he put his free arm around her shoulders. "Hush, little girl, it's all right now. Of course I came."

Antonia relaxed into his embrace, her sobs slowing.

"What happened, Toni?" Natalie asked. "I hold myself to blame for having ever allowed Delamere to drive you alone in his carriage."

"He—He wanted me to elope with him," Antonia said. "I explained to him that I didn't think I felt that way about him, but he refused to listen to me. I don't understand why. I know I did flirt with him, but I didn't like it at all when he kissed me, and I told him that again and again."

"Delamere is a villain," Michael broke in angrily.

"He's a self-centered, idiotic man who believes that everybody must love him as much as he loves himself," Natalie said. "If he had been forced to admit that you weren't swooning at his feet, that would have been too big a blow to his view of himself. I also think, my dear, that he had notions of being married to a princess. He would have loved the prestige, and I think the money wouldn't have come amiss, either."

Antonia stuck out her lower lip. "Well, I don't know about the prestige, but there wouldn't have been any money. Carl Friedrich would have been furious to lose me as a matrimonial bargaining chip, and nearly every penny I possess is dependent on his good will."

"I doubt Delamere knew that, though," Natalie said thoughtfully, "and you still haven't told us what happened."

"I demanded that he take me back to the Court, but he refused. I suppose I could have thrown myself from the carriage, but that seemed a mistake, considering the speed at which we were traveling. Vincent didn't give me any opportunity to seek help, either. He'd arranged ahead for changes of horses all the way. They were always ready for us. I don't think we can have been more than minutes at any of the changes, so I awaited my best chance."

Natalie's lips curled in a smile. "We found Delamere," she said. "I gather that your chance came in the form of a vase."

Antonia laughed, her natural ebullience starting to bubble up again. "Eventually, Vincent decided that we needed something to eat, and he took me in to a private room. And then he tried to kiss me again."

She grimaced. "Actually, it was a bit frightening, because he began to talk about making sure that I had to marry him . . . well, you know what I mean. He was, um, trying to unbutton my dress and, and it was horrid, because he wouldn't stop when I asked him."

Something suspiciously like a growl sounded from Michael. "I am going back to kill that man," he said furiously.

Antonia turned to him. "You're very sweet, Michael, dear, but I really don't think you have to. In fact, I may have done so already, though I hope not. He was still breathing when I left. I did check."

"He's not dead," Natalie assured her, "though he may wish he were when he awakens. You gave his head quite a crack, my dear."

"Good," said Antonia. "He deserved it. He was being quite, quite horrid. Anyway, then I was worried that he might wake up, and come find me, so I ran out and started walking to the Court. I got a ride for a while from a nice farmer with a load of cabbages, but mostly I walked. It was taking me some time, because I was worried that Vincent might come after me, so I kept hiding whenever I heard a fast carriage."

"You're safe now, dear," Natalie repeated soothingly, holding her hands, and Antonia relaxed against her shoulder.

Natalie glanced over at Michael, who was still muttering about death being too good for the likes of Delamere. Their time for confession had been interrupted, and could not be resumed in Antonia's presence. So she was left with her wonder at this enigma with whom she had fallen in love.

"It is unconscionable, Josef! It is totally unconscionable!" shouted Michael, early the next morning, striding up and down the great stone-flagged kitchen.

Josef smiled fondly. "It sounds as if the little princess fended quite well for herself."

"She never should have had to do so," said Michael.

"No, she shouldn't," Josef agreed.

"I am going to challenge the man to a duel."

"You can't," said Josef. "You don't know where he is."

Michael whirled around. "What?"

"He sent a message for his valet, who packed his master's clothes and has left."

"The coward," Michael said scornfully.

"You should be relieved. It would be difficult for the butler to challenge him," Josef pointed out. "Please try, my prince, to think with your head for a minute. What would it do for your sister's reputation if you started fighting duels in her name? It would be bad enough if you were known to be Prince Michael, but as the butler . . . Well, the scandal would be immense."

Michael sobered, staring at him. "I suppose you are, as always, correct," he said reluctantly. "Natalie said something, too, about keeping this quiet."

Josef snapped alert. "Natalie?"

"The countess, I mean," Michael said hastily. He felt a deep flush rise to his face.

"Natalie?" Josef repeated.

Michael berated himself. How had he come to love a woman who did not even know his true identity?

"Michael? Michael!" Josef prompted.

Michael swung around, paced the length of the room, then paced back again. "Oh, all right," he said crossly. "Have it your way. Do you want to hear the whole absurd story? I'm in love, Josef. Can you believe that? I'm in love with a countess who thinks I'm a butler. So now what?"

Josef smiled smugly. "It's wonderful, my prince. Congratulations. I have had such high hopes for this day. Your troubles are over."

Michael stared at him. "Did I hear you correctly?" he

said. "My troubles are over? I'm impoverished and disinherited, a prince without a country, unable to protect even my own sister as she deserves, in love with a countess who believes I'm a butler, and you think my troubles are over."

"She's rich," said Josef. "She has a house of her own. You marry her. We all live at the dower house. You, me, Princess Antonia. Our troubles are over."

Michael laughed harshly. "Josef, you're crazy. I'm not going to live on a woman's money." He shook his head. "In fact, I don't see a way out of this mess at all."

"But, my prince . . ." Josef protested, crestfallen. "It's a splendid scheme. The countess adores your sister. You could all live together happily."

Michael swung around again, stalked down to the end of the room and stared into the dying embers of the fire there. When he had left Estavia, he had known there would be consequences to his actions, but he had not realized how bitter they would be. Circumstanced as he was, a penniless outcast from his own country, how could he possibly hope to marry? He was barely supporting himself, let alone Toni and Josef, and this job would have to end now that he and Natalie had become involved. He had vowed to make a home for his sister, and somehow he would, but that was as far as he could now aspire.

No, he realized painfully, marriage to Natalie was out of the question.

Chapter Nineteen

"*H*ow are you feeling this morning?" Natalie asked Antonia, as they strolled through the rose garden. She herself had hardly slept at all, and was feeling emotionally battered. The realization that she had fallen in love with her butler was a sobering one, since she could see no hope of any happy resolution to her plight. She would have to dismiss Michael, for there was no hope of them continuing as mistress and servant, and she did not know if she could bear the pain of such an action.

She had stayed in her room for much of the morning, and had only finally emerged when she felt she could hide there no longer. The walk through the garden had been her suggestion, made so she could avoid the rest of her guests, and especially avoid coming face to face with Michael.

Antonia laughed. "Me? Oh, I am quite recovered. When you think about it, it was all really quite exciting, wasn't it? To think of you and Michael charging off as you did to my rescue. It was all very romantic, actually." Pausing, she looked up at her friend, speculation in her sparkling green eyes.

Natalie saw an opportunity to find answers to some of her many questions about the elusive Michael Schmidt. He certainly was not an average servant, and she thought that was why she had fallen in love with him. "You seem to know Schmidt quite well," she said, testing the water. "I suppose that since he worked for your family . . . But still, I've wondered several times that you seem on such familiar terms with him."

Antonia giggled. "Oh, yes, well, I do know him quite well. It's just that . . . I'm not actually supposed to say . . . But, honestly, Natalie, I don't see that it could cause any harm to tell *you*. In fact, I'm surprised he hasn't told you himself."

"So there *is* a mystery," Natalie remarked, half to herself.

Antonia giggled again. "Yes, you could certainly call it that. It's a trifle complicated." She paused for a moment, then appeared to come to some decision. "I don't think I've ever shown you the miniature I have of my brother," she said. "Not Carl Friedrich, who's only my half brother anyway. He's a bit of a prig, and much, much older than I am, so I don't bother to carry a painting of him. Not that he's ever given me a picture of himself, actually. I'm talking about my other brother. My dearest, dearest Michael, who has always taken such good care of me."

"I'd forgotten your brother's name was also Michael," said Natalie slowly, a sudden wild notion filling her mind. Surely Antonia could not be implying. . . . "If you'd like to show me your brother Michael's picture, of course I'd be delighted to see it."

Antonia fished in her hanging pocket, and produced a tiny, oval picture case, ornamented in the Russian style with enamel and emeralds.

"See," she said, snapping the case open and holding it out for Natalie to take.

Natalie looked down, and felt her breath catch. She saw a painting of a black-haired man garbed in a dark green uniform, resplendent with silver lace and braid, a tall shako embellished by a spray of black ostrich feathers sitting on his knee. His face was stern and yet held traces of humor, and his steel gray eyes were looking straight at her.

He was the most handsome man she had ever seen.

He was also—quite unmistakably—a twin to her butler, Michael Schmidt.

"Exactly. My brother, Prince Michael, has been masquerading as your butler," said Antonia.

"But . . . but why on earth would he do that?" asked Natalie, unable to conceive of a rational explanation.

"He was asked to do so specially. By—by . . . I'm not sure who. Your Prince Regent, perhaps. Anyway, Michael was specifically asked to investigate some problem. Traitors, I suppose."

"Here at Amesworth Court?" asked Natalie in disbelief. The thought of traitors overrunning her estate was difficult for her to imagine.

"Apparently so. I don't know many details. Michael felt it necessary for security to keep those private."

Natalie knew that her mouth was slightly ajar and feared she must look an idiot, but this was all too much to absorb.

"Antonia," she said, "I'm sorry, but I think I must leave you. I am suddenly feeling quite faint. I'll—I'll see you later."

Without waiting for a reply, she picked up her skirts and fled the garden.

Antonia sat down on a bench and admired a rose bush, feeling rather smug. Of course, she shouldn't have breached Michael's confidence, but she still felt it had been the right action to take. The two people she cared for most in the world were clearly falling in love with each other.

For days she had been covertly observing Michael and

Nini, and last night the charged atmosphere between them had been most marked. Though they had hardly spoken to each other, every look they exchanged, every time they pointedly spoke with her rather than each other, had been filled with underlying meaning.

She hoped Nini had gone to find Michael. That would be perfect. Now that Natalie knew he was not a lowly butler, surely she would fling herself into his arms. Antonia decided that she would not return to the house just yet. She didn't want to interrupt anything promising.

She was becoming a little bored with looking at rose bushes, however. Rising from the bench, she left the rose garden and strolled down toward the lake and the edge of the American garden, which came quite close to the house on this side.

It was a beautiful day, perfect for strolling. She stopped to admire some swans that were swimming on the lake, then entered the winding paths of the American garden. As she was walking along, she heard a soft churring noise and was suddenly hit by a twig.

"What on earth?" she asked aloud, looking around.

The churring noise sounded again from above her. She looked up and saw a tiny red squirrel sitting in a tree, scolding her indignantly. She laughed. "I gather you think I shouldn't be watching you," she said to the squirrel. "Well, then, you shouldn't have told me you were here."

She noticed a stone bench a few feet off the path, almost hidden by some spreading rhododendron bushes, and sat down to enjoy the squirrel's antics. When she remained motionless, it eventually decided she was harmless and started hopping around, looking for nuts.

Antonia sat there quietly watching for nearly ten minutes before the squirrel scurried away. She was about to stand and walk back to the house when she heard voices behind her.

"Are you sure that we can be completely private here?" asked one man.

"Oh, yes, nobody ever comes here. And, anyway, everyone is at the house right now. I checked before I came out."

"You've likely bungled that as badly as you bungled the last task I gave you. As I have told you already, those last documents you gave me are useless. There is nothing there that Napoleon does not already know."

Antonia sucked in her breath. *Traitors!* She could have danced with jubilation. Michael might think her merely a silly child, but she had found the traitors he had been unable to locate.

Shrinking as far back onto the shadowed bench as she dared, she listened intently. She thought one of the men was definitely English, but was puzzled by the other one. He spoke English but with an accent that sounded familiar to her.

"I don't know why you requested this meeting," said the Englishman in a low, whiny voice. "I have already told you that I will return to London and procure further information."

The foreigner laughed sardonically. "I know you told me that, but I do not trust you, my friend. Also, there is now a new document that I need. I have received word that your Prince Regent has been persuaded to ask Prince Carl Friedrich of Estavia to refrain from arranging a marriage between his sister and Orlando Bonaparte."

Antonia gasped. They were discussing *her*. No wonder Michael had been investigating here.

The Englishman was not very good at his job, she thought disdainfully. He was being scolded by the other man.

"*Ach, Gott in Himmell . . .*" said the foreigner and let loose a flood of contemptuous German.

Antonia stiffened. It had been a number of years since she had been home to Estavia, but when the man spoke German, she immediately recognized an Estavian accent. No wonder they were discussing her, then. She wondered whether Michael knew who the Estavian was, or even that an Estavian was involved. She didn't like the sound of him.

He was dismissing the Englishman now, speaking once again in English. He was telling him that he must procure more documents, the correct ones this time. He left then, stalking away. She shrank back into her alcove, but he was following a path that did not pass her.

The Englishman was still there, however, and she realized that it would be wonderful if she could get a glimpse of him. She would have much to report to Michael if she did. She crept very quietly off her bench and tiptoed around the bend in the path toward where the voices had been coming from.

She ran straight into someone.

He grabbed her by the arm. "What in hell are you doing here?" he shouted.

Antonia straightened and took a good look at the Englishman. It was Mr. Horace Poricy. She gasped. She found it unbelievable that the fat dandy could be a traitor.

"That was *you* selling secrets to the French?" she asked.

He scowled, and his grip on her arm tightened. "What did you hear?" he asked.

Antonia realized to her dismay that she had been indiscreet. "Not very much," she said, trying to retrieve the situation.

"Entirely too much, I think," said Poricy. "I certainly can't let you go back and tell anyone what you heard."

Antonia stared at him. "How are you going to prevent me?" she asked.

"I'm going to have to take you to Ireland with me."

"I don't think so," Antonia said furiously, wrenching herself from his grasp.

She tried to dodge around him and run down the path toward the house, but he grabbed her once again. Holding her with one hand, he pulled a small pistol from a pocket of his coat.

"Hold still," he said breathlessly.

Antonia decided that this was one of those cases where discretion was definitely the better part of valor. Mr. Poricy was very disturbed, and she certainly didn't want the pistol to go off while it was pointing at her. She held still.

Poricy stripped off his cravat and tied her wrists with it. "I can't believe this," he said angrily. "Why were you eavesdropping? I am ruining this cravat. It will never be wearable again."

"Why are you going to Ireland?" Antonia asked.

"I have to escape the count," Poricy muttered. "It's the only way I can think of to do so."

"You have a pistol. Could you not have disabled him with that? Or is it only women you dare use it on? You really aren't a very good traitor," she said.

His face grew purple. "Don't call me a traitor," he said sharply.

Deciding that perhaps it would be better to remain silent, Antonia held her tongue. And when he motioned with the pistol that she should walk along the path, she did as he told her.

Natalie sat in her boudoir, staring out the window at the lake. No matter how she attempted to order her thoughts, she was finding it extremely difficult.

She had fallen in love with a man who didn't exist. There was no such person as Michael Schmidt the butler. Was she in love with Prince Michael of Estavia? She had no idea. She didn't know that man.

Panic was coursing through her. Up until a month ago, she had thought she knew exactly where her life was leading her. She would have a controlled, quiet life as the dowager countess, mistress of her own little domain of the dower house. She would read and garden and embroider. She would visit with her friends. She would be content. It had all seemed so easy and practical.

From the moment she had met Michael Schmidt, or Michael whatever-his-name-was, her safe, secure world had been turned topsy-turvy. Now, she found her predominant emotion was anger. She didn't want her life turned upside down. How dare Michael stir up all her emotions in such a way?

But this was ridiculous. Surely she could put him out of her heart as easily as he had entered it. Yes, they had shared a few kisses, and she fancied herself in love. But what good did love do anyone, anyway? Her experience had shown that it frequently led to pain. If she had any sense at all, she would dismiss her supposed butler, cancel this ridiculous house party and move into the dower house tomorrow.

With that thought in mind, she stood and rang for her maid. She washed her hands and face and let Gwyneth straighten her hair, then sallied forth to see how her guests were faring.

As she walked down the stairs, she heard a commotion at the front door. The footman on duty opened it, and Max hobbled in, aided by one of the gardeners. His usually shining boots were smeared with mud, and grass stained his pantaloons.

"Max!" cried Natalie in horror. "What happened?"

He grimaced with pain. "Natalie, I'm sorry."

"What? Max, what's wrong?"

"I've sprained my ankle, obviously, but it's much worse than that. We have to speak in private, Natalie."

Natalie stared at him, wondering what could have happened. She turned to the gardener, who was still standing diffidently. "Thank you, Jim, for the aid you've given Mr. Chesney. You may go now."

With the aid of Percy the footman, she helped Max hobble into the library. They sat him down in a chair and propped his foot on a stool.

"Percy, find Lucretia," Natalie directed. "Tell her that we need bandages." She looked at Max's drawn face. "And some hartshorn, I think."

"No, no," Max protested. "No smelling salts. Brandy will do."

"All right," Natalie relented. "Percy, pour Mr. Chesney some brandy and then you may go and find Miss Dillerby."

The footman brought a small glass of brandy and left.

"Now, Max, what has happened?"

"Princess Antonia has ridden off in a closed coach with Horace Poricy. I saw them from a distance when I was walking. Poricy was pushing the princess along. I tried to cry out to them, to speak with them, but I fell down a bank and sprained my ankle."

"Oh, my heavens, Max! You can't be serious."

Max's face was woebegone. "I have failed you, Natalie."

"Oh, heavens, no, Max. Thank heavens you saw what you did. I just hope your ankle is all right. Let me take a look at it."

"No, no, Natalie. You must consider what to do about the princess. Lucretia will see to me, and perhaps you could send Josef to me."

"What *am* I to do?" Natalie asked.

Max, for once, was without a ready answer.

Then Natalie realized the answer herself. "Michael!" she cried.

Max stared at her. "What?"

"It's quite amazingly complicated, Max. I *will* explain,

but later. Now, you just sit here with your foot up until Lucretia comes."

She ran out of the library and saw Lucretia bustling toward her, equipped with bandages and a large bottle of smelling salts, followed by Percy.

"Oh, thank you, Lucretia. Max is in the library. Percy will take his boot off for you. I hope I can return soon."

She ran through the green baize door and down the stairs to the butler's pantry. Michael was sitting with his feet up on another chair, chatting with his alleged cousin Josef Stern, who was perched on a table.

She flung herself into the room. "Michael! Michael, Horace Poricy has abducted Antonia."

Both men jumped to their feet.

"What did you say?" Michael asked.

"Max just told me that he saw Antonia pushed into a closed carriage by Horace Poricy." She glared at Michael. "This is absolutely ridiculous. Things like this don't happen in my household. I have always led a calm, orderly existence, and now . . ." She stopped to take a breath. "Now . . . Well, look at it. Two abductions in two days. I won't stand for it. It's all your fault. It must be your fault, coming here with your spying."

Michael stared at her oddly. "Whatever do you mean?" he asked.

She felt a sudden, unreasoning longing to stamp her foot. Calm, controlled Natalie stamped her foot and it felt amazingly good.

"Pretending to be a butler," she said furiously. "Sneaking into my quiet, well-ordered household and turning it upside down looking for traitors. How dare you do such a thing? I won't have it. I absolutely will not have it!"

Michael and Josef turned to stare at each other, and said with one voice, "Antonia!"

"Well, I told you it was Antonia. Why in the name of

heaven has Horace Poricy kidnaped her? This is ridiculous!"

Michael strode to her and placed a soothing hand on her arm. "Natalie, my dear, would you please accept that I have very little idea what you're talking about. Other than I suspect that my dear little sister has been babbling." His mouth quirked. "I suppose I can assume at this point that you are aware she's my little sister."

"Yes, I do," said Natalie crossly. "And that's something else that we definitely need to discuss. A letter of recommendation from Prince Michael of Estavia, indeed! The impertinence of it!"

Michael gave her a shamefaced grin. "I suppose I shouldn't have done that, but I don't think you understand the circumstances that—"

"Indeed I do *not!*" Natalie said. "I have no idea why you or anybody else could possibly have thought that there would be traitors lurking around my house. Honestly!"

"But—"

She rode over Michael's hesitant interjection. "Who did you think the traitor was? Me, perhaps? Or Cousin Max? Oh, no, I have it—Cousin Lucretia! Of course, that's who it must be. Unless you suspect one of my guests?"

"I'm trying to tell you," Michael said, "that I don't think anything of the sort. This whole ridiculous notion of espionage was a fantasy of Antonia's. And if you would just give me a few moments, I will attempt to explain everything. However, I think we should make preparations to rescue Antonia first."

His voice of reason penetrated to Natalie. She calmed down long enough to take a good look at him, and the sight was enough to reassure her. No matter who he was, Michael was a man she could trust.

She sighed. "Of course, Antonia. You're right. That's our most important concern."

"Josef will go out to the stables and ask Hughes to ready a carriage and horses," Michael said crisply.

Josef nodded assent and left the butler's pantry. Natalie pulled a kitchen chair from the table and sat down.

"This sounds as if it could be a long story," she said, "but I think it's one I deserve to hear."

"It's really a very short one," Michael said. He smiled wryly. "I'm afraid that the real answer is considerably less romantic than espionage. It's a simple one of money, unfortunately.

"Last winter, my half brother Carl Friedrich, the ruler of Estavia, and I had a falling out on the subject of Bonaparte and what diplomatic position Estavia should take. I wanted to hold out against Bonaparte at all costs. Carl Friedrich wanted conciliation. Unfortunately, our disagreement ultimately led to my exile from the country, and since what money I have is tied up in my estates in Estavia, I was left penniless.

"I'm afraid that I was forced to seek employment to support myself, my sister, and my manservant, Josef. The position as your butler immediately offered itself. But I didn't want to tell Toni the truth. You know how she is, I think. She would have instantly insisted on joining me in a garret. I wanted to keep my reasons a secret from her. I'm afraid that Toni's fertile imagination produced the rest."

Natalie stared at him. "Well, I suppose that does make considerably more sense than espionage." She glowered at him. "But it still doesn't explain the lies that you told me."

"Have you had anything to complain about in my performance as a butler?" countered Michael.

"Well, no, I haven't. But . . . but . . . well, there are other matters. . . ."

Michael's face flamed. "Yes, perhaps that was not well done of me. But, I had provocation. This is not quite the time or the place to discuss it, but surely you must realize

that any—um—liberties I may have taken were only in-
dications of the strength of my feelings."

Now it was Natalie's turn to blush scarlet. "Oh." She
turned her face away from him, then after a moment said
briskly, "We must be going. I'm sure Hughes will be ready
very soon. He must be getting quite used to these sudden
demands. Oh, I do hope all is well with Antonia. Surely
there is nothing fat old Poricy could do to harm her?"

"I hope not," Michael said grimly. "He'd certainly better not!"

"But why in the world would Mr. Poricy be abducting
Toni?" Natalie asked. "He never showed a moment's interest in her before. Surely *he* doesn't have in mind marrying her."

"Mr. Horace Poricy has no money left," Josef answered her, walking into the kitchen. "His valet says he
hasn't been paid in six months. All of Poricy's income is
used to pay his gaming debts."

Natalie and Michael turned and stared at him.

"Well, he's mistaken if he thinks marrying Toni will
help him financially," said Michael.

"Yes, but Poricy doesn't know that," Natalie replied.

Michael scowled. "It looks as if we have only one
choice, doesn't it?"

Natalie smiled in response. "You're right. Only one."

Within minutes, they were preparing to leave on yet
another rescue. Natalie requested that Josef assist Max,
but cautioned him to silence on Michael's identity.

"I have no idea what I'm going to say on that point,"
she admitted with a sigh. "However, I'm going to have to
deal with it later."

Chapter Twenty

*I*nquiries in Abbingford Magna sent them north again.

"Gretna Green once again, I suppose," said Michael as they turned on to the main highway.

"I suppose so," said Natalie. But looking up at his face, she saw a doubt that matched her own.

He glanced at her. "You don't sound certain."

"Something doesn't seem right, though I don't know what."

"Do you have another explanation?"

"No."

"Well, then we'll just have to wait and see."

Natalie felt an awkwardness between them that hadn't been there before. She found herself stealing glances at Michael, trying to reconcile her new knowledge of his true identity with the man she had grown to care for too deeply. Of course, though at most times he had acted the perfect butler, she had often sensed and responded to the discrepancies and oddities in his behavior. Now, the reasons for them were clear.

His manner had changed, too, she thought. Now that he had cast off his disguise with her, she sensed a dash and a deeper sense of derring-do finally unleashed. She found it unsettling. She had long favored stability over excitement, and exiled princes forever on the trail of errant princesses didn't promise much stability.

"I think I'm still owed more of an explanation," she said, a little more sharply than she intended.

He glanced at her and arched one dark eyebrow in an inquiring fashion.

"What did you mean when you said you'd been exiled from your country over a disagreement with your half brother?"

"There was a rebellion," he said slowly, as if picking and choosing his words. "Bonaparte asked for a levy of troops, you see, for his march to Russia. I have never agreed with Carl Friedrich's policy of conciliation with the emperor of France, but I have always respected him as the ruler of our country. However, I could not risk my people dying in a foreign war without objecting."

He fell silent for a moment. "I made a mistake, I believe," he said reluctantly, "in speaking my thoughts aloud, not just to Carl Friedrich, as I felt I had to do, but elsewhere as well. My convictions were well known in our country, and the people knew I was in disagreement with my brother. They too did not want to send their young men to war in a strange country."

"I can understand that," Natalie murmured sympathetically, her heart wrenched by the pain in his voice.

"And so, one night, when Carl Friedrich was away from the capital, there was a rebellion. The people wanted to wrest Carl Friedrich from the throne and set me up in his place. I could not allow that to happen. He is my brother, after all. I never, never intended such a result."

"So what did you do?" she asked.

She thought he barely heard her, so buried in the past was he. "I hope I never have to endure such a night again. The mob was preparing to storm the palace in Stellberg.

Blood would have been spilled on the stones of Stellberg, spilled in my name." He shuddered.

"And so?" she asked.

"So I left. I wanted to go directly to Carl Friedrich, but I was advised against that. Count Rittenauer, who was our father's most trusted advisor before he was Carl Friedrich's, counseled me it was the wrong move. He told me that he agreed with me and my concerns. He promised that he would better plead my case with Carl Friedrich, and that I should absent myself from the country until the furor died. So I left. I believe now that was another mistake."

Natalie's heart ached at the sorrow in his voice, but she was afraid as well. This tormented story of darkness and bloodshed and the fate of thrones was not what she had bargained for when she had first been attracted to plain Michael Schmidt.

The curricle lurched sharply around a corner, and Natalie grabbed a side. She looked over at Michael. He was driving very fast now.

He seemed to sense her gaze, for he glanced over, giving her a quick smile.

"I'm sorry. Was that too fast for you? I *am* worried about Toni, you know."

"I am, too," she admitted, experiencing relief at the change of topic. It was easier to focus on the present concern than on what they might feel for each other and where those feelings could possibly lead. "I'm concerned there's something we don't understand happening," she continued. "I can't imagine Poricy as a suitor of your sister's."

"So you think they're not heading to Gretna Green?" Michael asked sharply.

"I can't decide," Natalie admitted. "Yet if they're not headed there, I have no idea where they would have gone. London seems unlikely."

"We must pursue this trail for a while at least," Michael decided. "It is the only lead we have."

So, despite their doubts, they followed the same route as the previous day. Michael inquired at the first staging stop. The grooms told him that a fat gentleman answering to Poricy's description had prearranged to change horses there and had passed by in a closed carriage that afternoon. A stable boy had noticed a young woman sitting in the carriage.

As soon as his own horses had been changed, Michael thanked the grooms and set the curricle in motion.

"So they are heading north," Natalie said.

"Let us hope we continue to hear word of them," he replied.

At each staging stop, the answer was the same. A fat gentleman in a closed carriage had passed through that afternoon. The miles ticked past until they were once more in Gloucester. There, pulling into the coaching inn, they saw a carriage in the yard.

Michael let out a shout, then had to soothe the frightened horses. "That's Poricy's," he said as soon as he could. "I recognize it from your stables."

"They must have stopped to eat," said Natalie. She giggled nervously. "Even on an elopement—or whatever this is—I can't imagine Horace Poricy missing a meal, can you?"

Michael smiled. "He certainly was one of Cook's biggest admirers."

Barely restraining his eagerness, he helped Natalie down from the curricle, then charged into the inn, Natalie hard on his heels.

Michael confronted the surprised innkeeper. "Have you seen a fat old man and a dark-haired young lady?" he demanded peremptorily.

The landlord looked startled and disapproving. Natalie

realized that while Michael's attitude had become decidedly princely, his dress was still that of an upper servant.

She intervened hastily. "I'm looking for my young cousin," she improvised. "She left home rather . . . um . . . precipitately, and I wish to speak with her."

The landlord thawed. "Oh, yes, milady. There is a dark-haired young lady here. She's up in my private parlor with her escort."

Michael snorted and charged up the stairs. Natalie ran after him, feeling a distinct sense of déjà vu.

The parlor door was unlocked and Michael slammed it open. Horace Poricy was lying beside the fireplace, unconscious. By his head lay the shattered remains of a vase and a scattering of sodden flowers.

Michael's jaw dropped in disbelief.

Natalie laughed. "Toni. I think I'm coming to recognize her *modus operandi*," she said. "Your sister does seem to have a certain . . . shall we say a distinctive . . . way of dealing with unwanted suitors, doesn't she? I suppose she's on her way back to the Court by now."

Michael grinned. "She is an enterprising chit, isn't she? Well, come along. I suppose we'd better inquire in the kitchens and the stables, ask if anyone saw her leave. And yes," he added in a resigned tone, "you may request that the innkeeper summon a doctor for Poricy."

"What!" Michael grasped the little stable boy by his shoulders, shaking him as a terrier would a rat.

"Michael, Michael!" Natalie grabbed his arm. "Michael, listen to me. This is not the child's fault."

Michael let the boy go and shook his head. "I'm sorry. You're right." He fished in his pocket and found a shilling. "Here, lad. What else can you tell me?"

"The young lady, was struggling, like. But the gennlemun said she was his naughty runaway ward, and that she must come home with him. Mister, I swear he had a pistol. None of the others here would believe me, but I think he had a pistol sticking into her. He had his arm wrapped around her, caring like, but I'm sure there was a gun in his sleeve. Furrin gennlemun, he was," he added, apparently seeming to think that this might explain the gun.

"What!" thundered Michael. Horace Poricy was upstairs unconscious, and this clearly was not Poricy being described. Who could have kidnaped Antonia now?

"I think he was a furrin gennlemun. He talked a little funny. Bit like you, sir, actually, 'cept he had these long, thin scars on his face."

"He had scars? And a gun? Pointed at the lady?" Michael was looking very grim.

"Yes, sir. I think so, even if none of the other grooms believed me. He had a huge black carriage—"

"A black carriage!" said Natalie.

The stable boy and Michael turned to stare at her.

"I saw one going the opposite direction from us on the post road as we came this way. I remember it distinctly."

"Well," said Michael tersely, "we're going after them."

Natalie was feeling deadly tired, and the world was swirling around her. The evening was closing in, and they had been driving all afternoon. Added to that, the day before had been trying, and she had slept little overnight. At one of the inns where Michael had stopped to inquire after a black coach, they procured some bread and cheese to take with them, but that was all they had had to eat all day. She leaned her cheek against Michael's broad shoulder, gathering strength from him. He seemed indefatigable, although surely the amount of driving he had done over the last few days must be exhausting.

Luckily, on such a balmy summer evening, there was no shortage of people out and about, and many of them had noticed the big black carriage. Michael and Natalie were able to trace it even when it turned off the post road about five miles short of Abbingford Magna. This close to the Court, Natalie knew the countryfolk and she got very accurate answers.

"Strange," she said, after interviewing one of her tenant farmers, who was out in a field. "I'd say he was heading for the back edge of Long Wood. There's not much there except a barn no longer in use."

"A barn?" asked Michael. "I've been wondering. It seems to me that this mysterious gentleman has a distinct destination in mind. There's no point in leaving the post road and wandering these narrow, winding lanes if he didn't. Does this lane lead anywhere else?"

"Not really," said Natalie. "Actually, if you follow it on, you end up back at Amesworth Court, but there are many more direct ways to do so. And I don't believe that this man was taking her to the Court. Not if she was as frightened as that stable boy said."

"I agree," said Michael. He reined in his horses and considered the lane and the surrounding countryside.

"Is that Long Wood there?" he asked, pointing at a mass of trees and tangled undergrowth across a field.

Natalie nodded.

"What happens if we cut across it? Can we approach the barn without being seen?"

"I think we could if we were careful," Natalie replied.

"I keep remembering what the boy said about a gun," Michael said in grim explanation, "and wondering if we're dealing with a madman here."

Natalie shuddered but said nothing in disagreement.

Michael wrapped an arm around her. "You've been very brave," he said, "and it's been a long day. So here is what we shall do. Will the farmer back there take the horses and carriage for a while?"

"Camford? Oh, yes, definitely. He's an Amesworth tenant."

"Good, then we're going to go there first. I'll leave the carriage and horses and you at the farm. Then I'm going to approach this barn on foot through the wood."

"On your own? You'll never find it," Natalie said. "The wood has strange little winding paths, and you don't know it at all."

"Maybe a boy from the farm . . ."

"Camford's boys are all little children. I'm coming with you. Antonia is my friend. I won't sit by while she's in danger."

Michael's protests lasted all the way to the Camford farm, but Natalie turned a deaf ear, and he finally subsided.

The sun was starting to set as they finally made their way on foot together across a cow pasture and into the wood.

Faced with the briery mass of undergrowth interspersed with nearly invisible trails, Michael was forced to admit that he needed a guide.

"I haven't come here of late, but I have a pretty clear memory of where the paths lead," said Natalie. "We're not as far from the Court as you might think. It's a good three or four miles by the lanes, but less than half that distance across the fields. I've walked to the Camfords frequently, so I think I can find our way."

She was understating the case. Unerringly she led them through the tangled maze until they glimpsed the dark silhouette of the barn against the evening sky.

"You have a good sense of direction," Michael said admiringly.

"It's always served me well," Natalie admitted. "What do we do now?"

"I'm still considering that gun," Michael said, pondering. "I don't want to put either you or Toni at risk in any way. I think we'll approach very quietly and assess the situation."

Leading the way, he went around the barn, keeping close to its walls as he approached the door. Natalie followed him quietly. She noticed that this time he made no effort to keep her back.

When they reached the door, he peered quickly inside, then motioned Natalie to retreat. She had barely enough time to glimpse Antonia sitting on a pile of straw, her hands and feet tied, and an unfamiliar man standing near her.

They regrouped at the edge of the wood. Michael's tanned skin was pale but his gray eyes were murderous.

"That bastard," he whispered furiously beneath his breath. "That bastard!"

"Who is he?" Natalie asked anxiously.

"I can't believe it," he muttered. "All this time, I thought he was on *my* side. What can he be doing? Is he kidnaping her for Carl Friedrich?"

"Who—" Natalie began again.

"Count Rittenauer," he said. "It's bloody Count Rittenauer. What the hell is he doing here?"

She had seldom heard such language used. She stared at him, picking up on the name. "Rittenauer?" she said. "Wasn't that the name of the man you mentioned? The man who had been your father's and then your brother's advisor?"

"Yes," he said bitterly. "That is exactly who he is. He said he agreed with me. He said he would plead my case with Carl Friedrich. What is he doing here in England, without my knowledge, holding a gun on my sister? He must be kidnaping her to take her to France."

Natalie shuddered. A dynastic marriage she could understand, though she might not agree with it. A forced one, by abduction at gunpoint to a foreign land—that was a terrifying thought.

"What are we going to do, Michael?" she asked.

"I have to think," he said slowly. "I can't rush in there and try to overtake Rittenauer when he has a gun. That's too risky. Antonia might get hurt." He considered briefly, then continued, "This is what we'll do." His voice was one of a man accustomed to command. "I'll stay here, keep an eye on Toni. Could you get back to the Court and summon reinforcements? I don't like the idea of your walking alone, especially with night coming on, but I see no help for it. I dare not leave Toni unwatched. Did you say you could walk to the Court from here?"

She considered the matter. "I could do that, but the way back to the Court leads across that field in front of the barn. What if Count Rittenauer were to notice me?"

"You're right about that," he admitted in frustration. "Then what . . ."

Natalie made a sudden decision. "I'll go back to Camford's and take the curricle," she said.

He looked at her with surprise. "Can you handle it?"

"If I take only two of the horses, I can," she said with resolution.

Her heart was pounding with fear at the thought, but she knew that she must attempt it. It had been nearly a decade—a lifetime, it seemed—since she had driven herself, but one of her earliest memories was of sitting on her father's knee in his curricle on a country road, holding the reins with his large hands over hers. By the time she turned twelve, she had been considered a notable whip, better than most grown women.

Michael looked her over assessingly, then gave her the credit of believing her.

"Good. Get back to the Court as fast as you can. Bring whoever is there. Josef, of course. And Percy, Oliver, and any grooms in the stable who might be able to comport themselves well in a fight. Josef will know. Ask him to choose them."

She looked at him admiringly. "You sound like a general mobilizing his troops."

"I am an officer of the Estavian army, and I have studied the arts of war. I should be able to execute a rescue of my sister from one armed man. Now, be on your way."

"Yes, sir," she snapped, with a mock salute.

He smiled, then suddenly swept her into a quick embrace. His arms were strong and reassuring around her, his lips possessive. She melted against him, her body instinctively molding itself to his, feeling his confidence giving her strength.

As quickly as he had seized her, he released her. "I love you, Natalie," he said brusquely. "Remember that. Now, you must hurry."

"Take care of yourself," she said softly. "I love you, too."

But Michael showed no signs of hearing. He was moving back toward the barn where his sister was held captive.

Natalie turned into the darkening wood.

Chapter Twenty-one

*L*eft on his own, Michael watched the quiet barn and thought of Natalie. How brave she was. Faced with a dangerous situation of which she had no experience, in which she was clearly uncomfortable, she was responding with courage and determination. With certainty, he knew this was the woman with whom he wanted to spend the rest of his life. How he would do so remained the only question.

Dismissing that concern as irrelevant to the moment, he scanned the barn again. There still was no sound from within. He set out on a careful tour of the exterior of the barn and discovered that the only exit other than the big front door was so overgrown with brambles that it was impossible to use. That determined, he crouched down behind a rickety hay wain, from which vantage point he had an unobstructed view of the front door, if not inside.

The minutes ticked by slowly. The light faded, and night started to draw in. Unused to inaction, Michael fretted and had to restrain his foot from tapping impatiently against the ground.

Just as darkness had almost completely settled, he heard the crunch of gravel around a bend in the farm road that led to the barn. Minutes later, a carriage drew up. Two large bruisers who looked more suited for a pugilism ring than the rural countryside jumped out. One carried a pistol.

Michael did not like the looks of this at all. He remained crouched behind the hay wagon, watching.

One of the newcomers disappeared inside the barn, while the other stayed with the carriage. In a moment, Rittenauer appeared, escorting Antonia, held closely by the arm. He had untied her, but in his other hand, as the stable boy in Gloucester had told them, he held a pistol. The bruiser followed close behind them.

"Get into the carriage," Rittenauer ordered Antonia.

She moved as if to obey, then suddenly jerked away and started to run for the nearby woods.

"Stop, or I'll shoot you!" Rittenauer ordered.

"Oh, no, you will not, Rittenauer," Michael said, emerging from behind the wagon.

Rittenauer turned and stared at him. "Prince Michael," he gasped.

"Yes, Count. It's Prince Michael."

"What—What are you doing here?"

"I think the question is what *you* are doing here," Michael said coolly.

"Michael," Antonia called, "Michael!"

Michael swore under his breath. "Antonia, run, dammit. Get into the woods."

One of Rittenauer's henchmen was circling around toward Antonia. The second was moving in his own direction, and Rittenauer had his gun pointed at him as well. There was little hope for himself but quite a lot for Antonia, if she would just obey him. He was afraid, however, that she would refuse to leave him.

Then he heard a noise in the distance, and his heart leapt. Could the reinforcements from the Court be arriving?

He chanced glancing away from Rittenauer as a flickering of light indicated a flare of torches across the field.

"I want you to walk away from that wagon with your hands in the air," Rittenauer ordered.

Slowly, Michael complied.

A muffled feminine shriek came from Antonia's direction. Michael cursed silently, and Rittenauer swung around. Michael saw to his dismay that Rittenauer's henchman had Antonia locked in a beefy hold.

"Rittenauer," called Michael in a low voice.

"Yes?" said Rittenauer, turning back toward Michael.

Michael didn't have many options. He needed to stall Rittenauer until his reinforcements arrived.

"I'll give myself in exchange for my sister," he offered, trying to buy time.

"I do not think," said Rittenauer coldly, "that would do me much good."

"What *are* you planning to do?" Michael asked.

"Your stupid little sister has overheard too much. I cannot afford to release her. And now I cannot afford to let you escape, either."

The man holding Antonia shouted a warning, interrupting them.

Michael realized that the Amesworth Court crowd crossing the field had nearly reached them. It was a motley group, led by Josef and Max, both waving dueling swords, a matched pair that Michael knew normally hung in the main hall at Amesworth. Max was limping, but he charged ahead valiantly. Behind them streamed a collection of footmen and grooms. Percy was clutching a frighteningly ancient blunderbuss that looked as likely to explode in his face as to hit its target. Other than that, the men were armed with only sticks, clubs, and torches. Then he saw Natalie, armed only with her courage, and his heart leapt despite his dismay that she had placed herself in danger.

Michael assessed the odds. Certainly numbers were on

their side, but little else was. Rittenauer had a deadly-looking pistol, and at least one of his party was armed as well. Their side had only one, most probably unsafe to use. They could rush Rittenauer and his flunkies and undoubtedly overcome them by sheer numbers, but it seemed inevitable that people would get hurt or killed in the process. If either Antonia or Natalie were injured, he would never forgive himself. He wished he'd explicitly ordered Natalie to remain at the house. Although it seemed unlikely that she would have obeyed.

The rescue group had halted in a ragged line, facing Rittenauer, his henchmen, and Michael and Antonia. Everyone was motionless, like players in a tableau.

Max shifted the weight off his injured foot, and Michael noticed again the dueling sword he carried. The seed of an idea took root.

"Rittenauer," he said quietly.

"Yes," growled the count.

"I think you must see you're outnumbered. Will you give yourself up?"

Rittenauer's gun was still cocked and ready in his hand. He trained it once again on Antonia. "I will not, Prince Michael." In the dim light of the flaring torches, the dueling scars on his cheeks stood out, giving his face an almost reptilian look.

"I'll fight you for our lives," Michael offered. "A test of skill. Single combat. The best man wins. A duel, Rittenauer. See, we have the swords right here—that matched pair that Josef and Mr. Chesney are carrying."

The pistol didn't waver. "Why should I use a sword?" asked Rittenauer. "I have a gun."

Michael laughed. "I thought you were Estavia's greatest duelist, Rittenauer. What is your boast? I've heard it. Fifty-nine duels fought, and you've never lost one?" He paused, contempt in his tone. "Are you afraid to lose now, Rittenauer? Are you afraid of me? You know my reputation as a swordsman."

He could see anger dawning in Rittenauer's eyes, a moment of hesitation in the hand that held the gun.

"I think you're afraid, Rittenauer. I think you don't believe you would win. There are those who say I would master you, Rittenauer, if we were ever to fight. You've heard them, haven't you? I have. If you are certain you can defeat me, then why are you hesitating? You have nothing to lose."

The veins in Rittenauer's forehead were standing out. The dueling scars had turned a shiny red.

"I will not stand here and be insulted. I could beat you with my right hand tied behind my back. You fight your prissy little fencing matches and believe you can best a real man in a real duel. I'll show you. Give us those swords."

Concealing his elation, Michael strode to Josef and Max. Max looked horror-stricken.

"What is going on here?" he demanded. "How does a butler know anything of duels or fencing?"

"You heard what Rittenauer called him," said Natalie quietly from behind. "Cousin Max, this gentleman is Prince Michael of Estavia."

Michael bowed. "Prince Michael Rupert Franz Peter von Stell, at your service, sir," he said. "Now, your sword, please."

Max's rubicund face was bewildered, but he handed over the sword. Josef handed him the other one.

Michael chanced a quick glance at Natalie. Her eyes were wide with fear, but she gave him a quick, supportive smile.

He turned back to Rittenauer, feeling like a medieval knight whose lady had knotted a favor around his arm.

"Put your pistol on the ground, Rittenauer, and you can have your choice of the swords."

He held his breath as Rittenauer slowly, with some hesitation, bent and placed the pistol on the ground. Then, with great ostentation, he checked both swords for flaws and selected one.

Michael took the remaining sword, and both men removed their shoes, as was traditional. The onlookers were forming a rough circle around them, leaving space to fight but also setting the boundaries of the dueling field.

Michael felt the familiar weight of the sword settle into his hand, felt the rightness of the hilt pressing against his palm and fingers. He sank into the fencer's pose, legs bent to allow maximum acceleration at any moment, his left arm held up and to the side to act as a counterbalance when he thrust.

The two men circled, testing the ground, accustoming themselves to the uneven grassy hummocks and the flaring of the torches. Both men advanced in a quick flurry, testing each other. The swords rang out, and they retreated as quickly as they had advanced. They had acquired a first feel for each other, for the strength of the other's grip.

Again and again they circled, occasionally coming together in a brief beat and riposte of steel ringing on steel. Rittenauer was good. Michael had never had any doubt of that, but he was also confirming what he had believed all along. He might just be slightly better. Rittenauer was a little too rigid, a little too rule-bound, but mostly a little too certain of his own invincibility. That was his failing.

As they continued to test each other, Michael was formulating a plan. It was a risky one that involved a certain amount of pain for himself, but Rittenauer had very few weak points and Michael dared not risk losing.

He waited, controlling himself, keeping himself reined in until he sensed the right moment. And then he faltered, letting his guard slip slightly. Rittenauer's sword flashed, aiming straight at Michael's shoulder. At the last instant, Michael recovered his guard and deflected Rittenauer's blade, but it was too late. The point grazed his upper arm, tearing through sleeve and skin.

As blood dripped from the cut, Rittenauer uttered an animal cry of triumph. "First blood, von Stell. First blood to me! Ah, you'll rue the day you insulted me."

In his triumph, he let his attention lapse briefly from his own sword—the moment Michael had been anticipating. Ignoring the pain of the slash to his upper arm, he seized all his strength and funneled it into a powerful lunge, flicking his blade up and over Rittenauer's in a rotating motion that pulled the sword from the count's hand and sent it spinning across the circle. Michael's own sword continued on in its path, straight at Rittenauer's throat.

At the last moment he stopped his forward momentum, halting just a hairsbreadth from piercing the count's skin.

Rittenauer froze, his breath coming in gasps.

"First blood, Rittenauer, but not last blood," Michael growled. "I see you now for what you are, a weak, puling coward who has betrayed his own country. Who is paying you for what you've done?"

The breath hissed out of Rittenauer. "Bonaparte," he whispered.

Michael could feel his fingers tightening on the sword. The longing to plunge it into the count's throat was nearly overwhelming.

"And what is he paying you?" he asked evenly.

"I would be a marshall in his army, and ruler of Estavia under him. I have a right to it. The blood that runs in my veins is as noble as any von Stell's."

"And you think Bonaparte cares how royal your blood

is?" Michael laughed. "When his is as common as any in Europe? Well, we'll never know if he would have redeemed his promise, will we?"

"Don't kill me," Rittenauer begged. "Don't kill me."

"The temptation is quite overwhelming," Michael said, "but I am not going to do so. There are ladies present. Also, I think the British government may have some questions they would like to ask you."

"Josef," he called without turning, "did you bring any rope with you?"

"Of course I did, my prince."

"I knew I could rely on you, Josef. Tie his hands together behind his back. And I think you'd better loop some rope around his ankles, also. We don't want to risk his running."

That task accomplished, Michael turned to discover that Natalie had retrieved Rittenauer's pistol from the ground and had his two henchmen under watch. They were but paid employees, and willing to plead for clemency. Michael directed that they be tied up, too, though he doubted the British government would have much interest in them. They would probably be released once it was determined whether they knew anything of import.

A shriek came from Antonia, and then she was plastered against him, laughing and crying and kissing him all at the same time.

"Michael, you were wonderful! You were amazing! And so this man is Count Rittenauer. I thought he seemed familiar, but I couldn't quite remember where I'd met him. I must have been no more than twelve the last time I saw him. Did you know that he's buying secret documents from the British? From Mr. Poricy! Did I help you find your traitors?"

Michael laughed and hugged her, letting her stream of

commentary flow, relieved beyond measure that she was safe once more.

He searched the crowd for Natalie and saw her standing silently beside Maximilian Chesney. She had given the pistol to Max, and something about her stance worried him. She was so rigid, and there was a coldness about her he had never seen before.

Chapter Twenty-two

*T*he excitement had died down, and practical Natalie was left to deal with the resulting disorder. The bound Count Rittenauer had been put under the guard of two excited footmen who had been armed with the captured guns. Once Antonia's tale had been told, Michael and Josef Stern had driven north through the night to retrieve Horace Poricy, which turned out to be an easy task. The two had returned with their captive, then departed the next morning for London in Natalie's best traveling coach, intending to deliver Rittenauer and Poricy to the proper authorities.

Michael had been willing to concede that this might be a matter for the local Justice of the Peace, but he felt that, given Poricy's tale of stolen documents handed to Napoleon, it would be better to take the traitors directly to the Horse Guards.

So, in the early dawn light, Natalie and Antonia had stood waving good-bye. As the morning lengthened, the various house guests stumbled down for breakfast, and by the end of the day they had started to arrange to take their leave. Emily Seabury was clearly perturbed at the thought of danger lurking in their midst, but the other guests seemed merely to feel that the news of captured traitors had put a period to the festivities. Aunt Abbie and

Aunt Gracie lingered on another full day before noticing that they were the only visitors remaining, and they began arranging their own departure.

When all the guests had departed, Natalie felt wrung out. She retreated to her boudoir and collapsed on the chaise longue with her feet up. Her eyelids drifted shut, but every time she closed them, that terrible moment when Count Rittenauer had drawn blood from Michael's arm appeared before her.

Finally, unable to rest, she rose and rang for Gwyneth. She would change and take a walk. Perhaps the peace and serenity of the woods beside the lake would soothe her. But even as she tugged on the bell pull, she heard a commotion in the circular drive below her window. She jumped. Surely it could not be Michael returning so soon.

Crossing the room, she peered out the window and saw an unfamiliar man of about thirty and a younger woman emerging from what was most likely a hired coach.

"No," she said desperately, as the truth dawned upon her. "No! Not today. I don't think I can meet the new earl today."

Of course, given the tendency for troubles to come when they were least needed, it was indeed the new earl and his wife. Despite her exhaustion, Natalie summoned up the energy to make the necessary efforts toward entertainment.

"Not, of course, that you need any welcome to your own house," she said to Lord Amesworth, who immediately demanded that she call him Cousin John and insisted that she consider the house hers as well for as long as she liked.

He was solemn and serious and very interested in the details of running an English estate. Kitty Chesney was more vivacious, a pretty young woman with an engaging manner.

She immediately took Natalie to her heart and within minutes was confiding that they had one more piece of news. "I have started a child. I realized it on the voyage here. We thought it was just seasickness for quite some time, but instead, by spring there may be a new heir."

Natalie felt a pang of envy. She had sometimes dreamed of little boys and girls running through the long corridors of Amesworth, but it had been her children she was dreaming of. Upon receiving Kitty's news, she was even more determined to move into the dower house immediately. There was no reason she should not. The preparations were nearly complete.

The following morning, Natalie was standing in the front drive with Antonia, overseeing the packing of her personal possessions into a wagon for the short journey to the dower house, when she once again heard the sound of carriage wheels on the driveway.

This time it must be Michael, and she realized they had never discussed, in light of his true identity, how they really felt about each other. Perhaps he didn't feel very much for her at all. He was a prince, as high in rank above her as she had imagined him to be below her. A princely marriage, after all, was an affair of state. All things considered, she thought it might be best to remain reserved.

The carriage drew up, and Antonia ran shrieking across the expanse of gravel and into Michael's arms the minute he jumped from the carriage. Natalie stood to one side, admiring how they looked together. She wished she had Antonia's joyful lack of inhibition, but she didn't think it was a part of her makeup. At that moment, though, she felt very lonely and left out.

Michael looked over Antonia's head, as if searching for something. Seeing Natalie standing back, he smiled and beckoned to her.

"Come over here," he called, his excitement plain. "I want my two favorite women to hear my news."

Natalie slowly crossed the gravel.

"Rittenauer and Poricy have both been imprisoned," he said, "and they will undoubtedly stand trial for espionage and treason. But I have something even more exciting to tell you. You'll never believe whom I finally met in person," he said. "The Prince Regent himself. I had written a letter to him asking for his aid with Antonia's and my plight, but he had not yet found the time to make a decision concerning us. However, when Castlereagh revealed to him my hand in Rittenauer and Poricy's capture, he became most interested. He was very kind to me and seconded my belief that Estavia should continue to resist Bonaparte.

"And listen to this. He has offered me a position in his government. I will be a special liaison to the courts of Europe that are still standing against Napoleon. He wants me to travel to Sweden as soon as possible, and there is even a chance I might continue on to Russia."

Natalie gasped. "But Bonaparte is invading Russia at this very moment," she said, the words torn painfully from her tight throat.

Michael beamed. "Yes, isn't it wonderful? Finally I feel that I have a real purpose in life again, a contribution to make to the world, and for my country, for Estavia."

A cold numbness was creeping through Natalie as she thought of Michael's purposely putting himself in harm's way, just as Giles had done. How dare he be so happy about it? Giles, she remembered, had been just the same.

"So you won't be returning to Estavia?" she said, mostly to say something.

Michael sobered. "No, not immediately, at least. It has become very clear that Count Rittenauer was actively lying to both my brother and myself. Possibly if I were to return to Estavia and apologize to Carl Friedrich, I could effect a reconciliation. But I don't think I wish to do so. I disagree too strongly with Carl Friedrich's stance."

And you still feel slightly bitter about it, too, Natalie added silently.

In a moment, though, he had recovered his exuberance. "I greatly enjoyed talking with the Prince Regent and his advisors," he said. "Lord Castlereagh is a very astute man, indeed. I believe that England will win this war eventually, and I will be proud to have played a part in achieving Europe's freedom from Bonaparte's oppression."

Antonia clapped her hands. "And we *did* find the traitors! I always knew you would. And I was so proud to play a part in that."

"Toni—" Michael said, then stopped. Natalie saw the play of emotions across his face, and guessed that he would never quite be able to set Antonia straight. She herself had often experienced the same confusion.

Antonia looked at her brother inquiringly. "Yes, Michael?"

"Toni, do you think that you could find something else to do for a few moments? An urgent errand in the house, perhaps?"

For once, Toni was completely acquiescent, grasping immediately the undercurrent to Michael's request. She flung her arms around his neck and gave him a quick hug. "Of course, Michael. Please be very romantic, my dear."

She turned and hugged Natalie, too. "Oh, Natalie, this is so exciting. You will have to tell me absolutely everything later." Then she danced across the gravel drive to the house.

Michael was grinning at his little sister's retreating figure. "Nothing like making it impossible for a man to be subtle," he said wryly. "Will you take a walk down to the lake with me, Natalie? I'd rather not be observed *too* closely by my inquisitive sister."

The hollowness in the pit of Natalie's stomach was deepening. Mutely, she took the arm he offered her, and they strolled down to the lake and into the American garden.

As soon as they were out of sight of the house, Michael turned to her exuberantly.

"Finally, finally, Natalie, I can ask you what I have been longing to ask for a month. You must know how I feel about you, and at last I have managed to re-establish myself in life. Natalie, now that I can support you, will you marry me?"

She was mute. Her fingers and toes felt like ice, and she couldn't move. She loved him, she knew. She loved him far too much. But she was also afraid. Afraid to risk heartbreak all over again. Faced with the thought of leaving the safety she had created for herself at Amesworth Court, knowing that Michael would be in constant peril, she found she could not do it. The depth with which she loved him made it impossible, for the greater her love, the greater was her fear of losing him.

As if from a distance she could hear Michael's worried voice, "Natalie? Natalie! What is it?"

He closed the distance between them, and took her in his arms. His lips covered hers, and they were as sweet as they had ever been, but she tore herself away.

"No," she said. "No! I cannot do it!" With a great, gulping sob, she turned and started quickly toward the house. Tears blinding her, she stumbled and nearly fell.

Michael, who had followed, caught her as she tripped, and pulled her close against him.

"Natalie, I don't understand," he said. "What can't you do? I thought you loved me."

"I do, I do," she snuffled miserably. "But I—I can't

leave all this. Everything I've done to make my life . . ." The tears were overwhelming her and she couldn't go on.

He released her, and a noticeable chill spiked his voice. "I see," he said. "Perhaps I should have chosen to return to Estavia. There you could have lived in a palace surrounded by obsequious servants. But I have made up my mind. I'm not going back. And, no, I can't offer you a life such as you have here. I no longer have a grand estate. I once lived in considerably more splendor than you do here, but I forfeited all that when I left Estavia. And let me tell you, Natalie, that if I had ever been faced with the choice between my estates in Estavia and marrying you, I would have chosen you."

"No," she said desperately. "No, Michael. It's not like that at all! It's that I—"

She stopped, realizing she was talking to his retreating back. He had walked away from her, leaving her no chance to explain herself. Her knees buckled, and she sank to a nearby bench.

Chapter Twenty-three

She was supposed to be happy.

Everybody else was happy. John and Kitty Chesney were settling in very well at the Court, and Kitty especially was deliriously happy as the baby inside her grew. She enjoyed Natalie's company, and frequently invited Natalie to tea, or popped over to the dower house to consult with Natalie on such matters as hiring a new butler, which had been managed with surprising ease. Max was happy, too, even though he was having to search for a new valet now that Josef had left with Michael. He got on well with John, for he remembered the younger man's father and enjoyed telling stories of their youth together. Even Lucretia was as happy as she had ever been. The dower house was smaller than the Court, and thus easier to heat and less prone to drafts.

Natalie, on the other hand, was finding she was not happy at all. Whatever she tried to settle to doing, she could not seem to enjoy. After the hustle and bustle of preparing the dower house to be habitable, her life seemed empty. Once she had spent hours every day on the estate accounts and longed for the time when she would no longer have to do them. Now, she missed the exercise they gave her mind, which sorely lacked occupation.

She was trying to get her garden into order, but there

was little interesting to be done in late August. Next spring would be different, of course, but right now she could only make interminable sketches of what she planned. She had ordered a few more furnishings from London, but they hadn't yet arrived. She had never liked needlepoint, which Lucretia did endlessly, and even the gossip of her middle-aged and elderly neighbors had started to seem narrow-minded and provincial.

Worst of all, however, were the visits from Kitty. The other woman was positively glowing from her pregnancy. Natalie found herself feeling sharp jabs of jealousy when the new countess talked of refurbishing the nursery or suddenly placed a hand in pleased surprise on her stomach, explaining that the baby had moved.

Of course, if matters had gone as Natalie had once supposed they would, it would be her sons and daughters to inhabit the nursery at Amesworth Court. But she found herself dwelling on another image—an image of a little boy or girl with dark hair and Michael's pale gray eyes, and of Michael himself leaning protectively over her gently swelling stomach to feel his baby move inside her.

In fact, Natalie was not happy at all. She was depressed and restless and unable even to sleep well. One morning, she was listlessly inspecting the garden and thinking about Antonia, who had departed, a bit tearful at leaving her dear Nini, with Michael and Josef. A letter from the girl waited inside, but Natalie hadn't had the courage to open it yet. Instead, she wondered whether she could perhaps transfer in some daffodil bulbs. As she considered the matter, a carriage pulled through the gate.

She looked up in surprise, then gasped as the footman who hurried out from the dower house helped down a thin lady of late middle age.

"Aunt Emilia," she cried.

Emilia Thorpe surveyed her up and down, then pronounced disapprovingly, "I see that your marriage did nothing to improve your hoydenish ways, Natalie. You have dirt on your dress, which looks to be three or four years old. I would think you'd be ashamed to receive company in such attire."

Natalie forbore to mention that she had not expected company, that when a person gardened it was quite usual to get slightly dirty, and that what was more she had worn an old dress intentionally, for that very reason.

A portly gentleman climbed down behind Emilia. "Good afternoon, Uncle James," she said resignedly.

"Harumph. Harumph," he said. "Stuffy little driveway you have here, Natalie. And what a small house this is. Why, there will barely be room for all of us to stay."

"All of you . . ." Natalie queried. "Oh, I see," she sighed as Jane and Raymond Hargrave descended from the carriage as well.

She brushed her hands down her skirt, defiantly leaving two more streaks of dirt. She saw Aunt Emilia frown and at once felt thirteen years old again. She supposed she should invite her unwanted guests inside but wished that she could avoid it.

"Jane had some most distressing stories to tell us of your behavior," Aunt Emilia said.

Natalie felt a familiar shudder of apprehension. It might have been years, but she remembered the drill well. First, Jane ran to her mother with complaints of her quarrels with Natalie. Next would come the verbal lashing in which the inadequacies of Natalie's nature and behavior would be laid bare. Then she would be forced to stand and listen to a damning description of her youthful and profligate parents, who had crowned their intemperate lives by the disgraceful act of dying suddenly and young, leaving no money to support their child, and forcing Uncle James, out of the goodness of his heart, to take Natalie into his household, only to see her corrupt her cousin with her impossibly bad manners.

Through this entire process, Natalie was forced to stand with bowed head, accepting blame for her and her parents' sinful ways.

In comparison, the caning that usually followed would seem mild. Uncle James did not believe in undue whipping for girls. It seldom lasted long, nor left broken skin or even much visible bruising. She had recovered eons ago from those few physical marks, but she found her soul still flinched from the verbal battering.

"Unfortunately, we were touring the Lake Country during the time of your house party," said Aunt Emilia, "but on our return we stopped to visit Jane, and she and Raymond informed us of how you held our family up to the ridicule of polite Society. She says"—here Aunt Emilia took a deep breath of indignation—"that you have been conducting an indecent and immoral affair with your *butler*. With a servant, Natalie!" She paused, clearly expecting Natalie's denial.

Natalie felt a surge of anger rush through her, the same anger that had supported her in her confrontation with Jane, but stronger now. She realized that she had repressed such anger for many years, since her first rebellious days in her aunt and uncle's home.

"I would rather," she said sharply, casting a look at Jane and Raymond, who hovered in the background, "conduct an affair with a cultured and sensitive man like Michael Schmidt than be a vicious cat married to a pedantic bore who sends everyone he meets immediately to sleep."

Aunt Emilia gasped.

Jane flushed a bright unattractive red.

Uncle James and Raymond harumphed in harmony.

And Natalie felt a most improper triumph.

"In fact," she added, "if Jane had bothered to stay and eavesdrop a little longer, she would have found out that the man using the name Michael Schmidt and serving as my butler is actually Prince Michael of Estavia."

Aunt Emilia's mouth opened, but Natalie did not allow her time to speak. Her blood was up, and she was feeling a heady sense of release.

"Not," she added, "that it is in any way any of your business!"

Aunt Emilia's jaw dropped, and she looked nonplused.

Natalie swept a look around the group. "My concerns are my concerns," she said, "and I will thank you to remember that. If I wish to conduct an affair with every servant I have, or . . . or . . . swim naked in the lake, then I have a perfect right to do so without requesting your permission. That is all. I think you had better leave now. I have far more pleasant things to do with my life than stand here being unjustly criticized and condemned."

Aunt Emilia was nearly purple with suppressed rage, but she seemed unable to form a single coherent word. After sputtering for a few moments, she turned around with an ostentatious gesture of disdain and swept her little flock back to the waiting carriage.

Natalie watched the carriage disappear down the drive. Her rage fading, she was left with a sense of liberation. She had confronted her worst fears—challenging her former guardians—and nothing had happened.

"Now," she said aloud to the empty air, "I am going to swim in the lake. I have *always* wanted to do that."

Natalie hadn't swum in years, but she found she still remembered something of the technique. Now she floated gently on the surface of the lake, wearing only her shift and reveling in the sense of freedom.

Finally, she understood that for years she had lived

with the fear of what *could* happen, and she had allowed that fear to rule her until it had become more terrible than anything that did happen.

The worst that could happen to her was not losing someone she loved to death, but permitting that fear to rule her life.

She had not eloped with Giles when her aunt and uncle forbade her to marry him because she was afraid of the consequences of defying them. Because of that, she had never known the joy of having married her young love. Yes, Giles likely still would have died, but if she had gone to Spain with him as he begged, they would have had two happy years together. The loss of that, she saw now, was the greater tragedy.

And now she had committed the same mistake again. She had sent Michael away because she was afraid of the perils that came with life and love itself. She had chosen to retreat into a shell, into what she had believed to be peace and contentment, and already she was living with bitter regret. For years she had run from emotions, and never fully realized it. She had never escaped her fear, not even when she married Alden and left her aunt and uncle's house. She had not escaped it until this morning, when she had finally confronted it and overcome it.

She had been so sure that she didn't possess the courage, and yet now that she considered the matter, courage had always come to her when she needed it. When Alden was ill, she had found the strength to tend him lovingly even as she raged internally at losing him. When Antonia's reputation had been at stake, she had found the courage to ride in the same kind of carriage that had killed her parents. And when Toni's life had been imperiled, she had even been able to drive such a carriage. Now, with her own happiness at stake, she needed to draw on that same bravery.

She stood up and waded out of the lake, the water pouring off her like diamond sparkles.

"I have made a mistake," she announced to the world, "and I am going to set it right. I am going to marry Michael." The thought sent a surge of joy such as she had never known racing through her. "I am going to marry Michael," she repeated.

Drying herself briskly, she dressed and returned to the dower house. It occurred to her that she had no idea where Michael was at this moment, but, riding on a wave of assurance, she knew that she would overcome such details.

On her little marquetry escritoire in her bedroom sat the letter from Antonia. She broke open the wax that held the cover closed with a feeling of certainty, knowing that within would be the very details she needed.

Brighton was bustling with people. The carriage, which Cousin John had kindly allowed Natalie to borrow from the Amesworth stables, moved slowly through the crowds. Natalie sat forward, gripping the seat as she had almost all the way from Amesworth, but she saw hardly anything. The fashionably dressed crowd, even the gigantic Oriental bulk of the Prince Regent's famed Royal Pavilion, passed in a barely noticed blur before her eyes.

She was terrified but equally determined that, this time, she would not let fear rule her. This time she was going to achieve her happiness. She was going to propose marriage to a man. It did help that he had already asked her once, but for all that it was still a frightening move. Michael had been very angry when he left her.

The coach turned into a small side street and stopped in front of a row house. The groom from Amesworth, who had been riding with Alfred, the coachman, jumped down to help her descend. "Alfred says this is the house, milady," he reported.

Natalie took a deep breath but stayed in the carriage. "Ring the bell, will you please, Thomas?" she requested calmly.

A middle-aged woman answered the door, and Natalie watched Thomas confer with her. The woman disappeared inside, and Natalie tried to summon the courage to leave the carriage.

Before she could force herself to do so, though, a blurred form bolted down the front steps and into the carriage.

"Nini, Nini darling, you're here! Did you get my letter? I've missed you so since we parted. You are so, so naughty, Nini dear. You made Michael very miserable, and I can't imagine why you would not want to marry him. He is absolutely the best of brothers, and I am sure he would be the very best of husbands, as well."

Natalie smiled faintly. Toni's barrage of words was, as always, slightly stunning. "I agree with you, Toni," she said softly.

Antonia drew away and stared at her. "You agree? That Michael would make you deliriously happy?"

Natalie nodded.

"Then why ever did you not tell him that? He was very, very upset, Nini. You have no idea how upset he was."

"I was a fool and a coward, but I see that now," Natalie said. "Is he here, Toni?"

The younger girl nodded. "He's upstairs. We have lodgings here, you know, just for a few days longer, until Michael leaves for Sweden. It's quite terribly expensive here, even this little house, but Michael has to consult with the Prince Regent daily, so we needed to be nearby. I think Prinny, as they call him, is paying for the rooms, actually. In fact, we were quite awfully lucky to get it, for Brighton is very crowded in the summer, but the Prince

Regent arranged something. Michael is doing some paperwork in the parlor right now," she babbled happily. "Let's go up directly."

"Would you let me go up by myself, Toni?" Natalie asked.

"Oh, of course," Antonia agreed. "I'll go and see Mrs. Brown in the kitchen," she volunteered. "She's teaching me how to cook. I think that's a useful thing to know, don't you?"

Natalie smiled but refused to allow herself to be deflected by Antonia's chatter. "Wish me luck," she said.

Antonia sobered and hugged Natalie. "All the luck in the world, my dearest Nini. Oh, I do hope you will soon be my sister-in-law, even if Michael was most dreadfully, dreadfully angry. Oh, and the parlor door is the first one on the right."

The staircase seemed very long and steep, though Natalie knew it was not unusually so. She could feel her heart thumping in her chest, and the sick feeling in her stomach was nearly overwhelming. She stopped halfway up the stairs to calm herself, but only felt worse. She decided this was quite the most frightening thing she had ever done in her life. Rescuing Antonia from a band of armed villains paled in comparison.

The door to the parlor was ajar, and she pushed it open very quietly. Michael was sitting at a desk by the window, and she could see only his profile.

She stood still for a moment, memorizing it, wishing that she could run her hands over every treasured line. She knew now that she would be willing to give anything, even all hope of safety and security, for the chance to spend even a few precious days and nights with him. She closed the door behind her and he turned at the sound.

"Natalie," he breathed, "what are you doing here?"

His eyes were hungry, drinking her in. She could almost feel his embrace from across the room. Her heart leapt in joy.

Then his expression abruptly turned angry, and she knew her mission would not be easy.

"What are you doing here?" he repeated coldly.

"I . . . I changed my mind."

"You changed your mind?" he echoed. "Might I ask why?" He picked up a penknife and sharpened a quill pen with quick, hard strokes.

She could see the anger in his every movement and it felt very hard to force the words up her throat and out of her mouth, but she had to find the courage. Her hands were icy and she squeezed them into nervous fists at her side. What could she say to win his forgiveness?

She said the only thing she could think of, the only thing there really was to say. "I love you, Michael," she said.

Slowly, he placed the quill and the knife down on the desk. He looked up at her, a guarded light in his eyes.

"Do you?" he asked. "Do you love me enough to marry me, even though I have no idea where I will be six months from now? Do you love me enough to come with me to Sweden and even further?"

A flare of joy surged through her, and the last piece of the puzzle slipped into place for her. She realized suddenly that she had not been frightened when they had been creeping round the barn together. Even when she had been driving a curricle for the first time in ten years, she had felt no fear. Only later, when she had been forced to stand to the side and watch Michael in danger, had she felt that fear.

"I'll do more than that," she said. "I'll never let you out of my sight. If you go to Russia, then I'm coming, too."

He crossed the room in mere moments, and she found herself deep in his embrace, the one place in the world where she felt truly at home.

"So you don't care if I can't offer you a palace?" he asked.

"Oh, Michael, I never did care what you could offer me, besides yourself. I was just a coward, afraid to lose you."

He looked down at her in surprise. "You, a coward? Why, Natalie, you're the bravest woman I have ever met."

"I wasn't before I met you, Michael. You have taught me courage. You gave me the courage I needed. I'm sorry that I wasn't able to see that before and I'm sorry that I couldn't explain it to you."

He frowned. "I think you did try to explain it, but I wouldn't listen. I shouldn't have stormed away like that. That's my besetting sin, you know. I sometimes act too quickly."

She looked at him fondly. "We must always be sure to listen to each other," she said.

"Always," he vowed, "but right now I know of something more important than talking."

He bent her nearly backward in an ardent kiss. She pressed herself against him, reveling in the feel of his muscled hardness through her thin muslin dress.

"Natalie," he murmured, "you can have no idea how I have burned for you every day that we have been apart."

"Oh, I can," she sighed, "for I have burned as well. But, Michael, there is still something I should tell you." She blushed, then realized she could not say the words aloud. Snuggling closer into his arms, she whispered them into his ear.

He smiled. "Ah, so that explains something that has always puzzled me about you." He kissed her once again.

"Natalie, my dear, I think this has definitely become a matter for a special license. I will go insane if I have to wait three weeks to make you my wife. And I must leave for Sweden in less than one week."

She smiled back at him, still blushing.

A knock sounded on the door and they stepped apart.

"May I come in?" Antonia called.

Michael sighed. "I suppose so."

"Well, I certainly hope that the two of you are engaged by now," Antonia said, bursting into the room. "What *has* been taking you so—"

She stopped, taking in Natalie's disheveled curls and blushing cheeks, and Michael's satisfied smile.

For once, Antonia looked nonplused, but not for long. "Hurrah!" she cried. "So you are getting married, then?"

"Are we, Natalie?" asked Michael intimately.

"Yes, oh, yes," she said fervently.